CNIU

ECIA CHAPTER 2

THE GOOD SIDE
OF MY HEART

THE GOOD SIDE OF MY HEART

Ann Rinaldi

5448

HOLIDAY HOUSE / NEW YORK

To all my good friends,
reporters and editors
in the newspaper world,
from whom I've learned so much.

The author would like to thank Mr. Joseph Schmeltz,
Director of the Mercer County, N.J. Wildlife Center,
for his friendship and assistance.

Library of Congress Cataloging-in-Publication Data

Rinaldi, Ann.
  The good side of my heart.

  SUMMARY: When, despite her father's disapproval,
sixteen-year-old Brie begins to date the handsome and
considerate Josh, she hopes that their relationship
will go beyond friendship until he reveals to her
that he is homosexual.
  [1. Interpersonal relations—Fiction.
2. Homosexuality—Fiction. 3. Prejudices—Fiction]
I. Title.
PZ7.R459Go 1987   [Fic]   86-46200
ISBN 0-8234-0648-2

THE GOOD SIDE OF MY HEART

Chapter 1

I first learned about Joshua Falcone the way you first hear a new song, in the background, not completely paying attention to it. You have to hear it several times before it takes hold in your mind. And that's where Josh was all my life. In the background. He was my best friend Gina's brother.

He had been away from our town, Waltham, since he was fourteen. In military school. Summers he always went to his and Gina's grandparents' in Boothbay, Maine. All I remember before those years was a lanky shy boy, two years older than Gina, who stayed out of our way whenever we were together.

They never fought, now that I look back on it. He didn't tease or torment her the way brothers usually tease and torment their sisters. Certainly not the way my brother, Kev, teases me sometimes. And he's fifteen years older than me. And a priest. No, Gina

always seemed like the older one when we were little kids. I noticed how protective she was of Josh.
But I always thought that was because he was so shy.

He came back to Waltham late in the summer before I started my third year at Waltham High. I knew
he'd been thrown out of Chittendon, the military
school in Pennsylvania. And I knew that it had something to do with a girl. Gina never told me that. She
never mentioned it at all. I found out about it
through the grapevine. And since Gina didn't volunteer the information, I never asked her about it. We'd
been friends since fourth grade and so I knew when
not to pry.

I was in Gina's house one day in late August. It
was hot and sticky and the central air was going.
Gina was not home when I got there. She'd just gone
out to run an errand for her mom. Their maid let me
in. Gina's father is a banker and they have lots of
money. My dad owns one of the daily newspapers in
the area, the *Journal*, and we're pretty comfortable
too. But we're less ostentatious about how we spend
our money. Good grief, with Kev a priest, I think
he'd disown us if we had a maid with a white apron
and cap like the Falcones do. Sure, we have Alma.
She's been with us as long as I can remember. But
she's almost part of the family.

Anyway, the maid said I should go into the living
room, that Gina would be right back and that her
mom was napping upstairs. She even brought me a
glass of lemonade. I was sitting reading my dad's

paper when I suddenly felt somebody looking at me. I looked up.

He stood in the doorway, halfway into the center hall. He was wearing cutoffs and sneaks and an old ratty faded oxford shirt. I noticed how frayed the collar was, but over it he wore a sweatshirt, gray in color, durable quality. It had the name of his military school on it. Chittendon, it said. In deep blue letters.

I gasped. My first impression was...tall, tan, easy smile, handsome! At first I couldn't place him. I hadn't actually seen him in years. I stood up. The paper dropped from my lap.

"Hello." He grinned at my discomfort.

"Hi."

We stood looking at each other. "I know you haven't seen me for a long time. I'm Gina's brother, Josh."

"Oh!" I was even more embarrassed. "I'm sorry. I didn't recognize you. I mean, I didn't know...I—"

"It's okay. I'm sorry I startled you. You're Brie."

"Yes." Who uses a word like that? Startled. He was blushing under the deep tan because I was staring at him with such brazen admiration, like a little teenybopper staring at a rock star. His smile widened, stretching something inside me beyond endurance.

"Hey," he asked, "do they know you're here?"

"Oh sure."

"Fine. Good. You'll be all right then?"

"I didn't know you were home. That's why I was so...startled."

"Sure. It's okay. No sweat. I just got home last night from Maine. I start school in a week, just like you. Waltham High."

"Oh. Well that will be nice."

"No it won't. It'll be miserable after Chittendon. But I went and got myself kicked out. I guess Gina told you."

"She didn't tell me anything."

"Well, it'll be all over town by the time school starts, so you might as well know."

My face was burning by that time. Because I couldn't keep from staring at him. I felt unable to pull my eyes away.

He was absolutely beautiful!

Everything about him was perfect. His blue eyes, his brown hair, his physique, his voice, his studied and casual indifference to himself and to the beautiful surroundings. I sensed at once that he was only a visitor there. That he belonged somewhere else.

He turned to go, and I saw his straight military bearing, the grace of his movements. He smiled again, never taking his eyes from me.

"You've grown up." He stood, facing me sideways, his hands thrust loosely onto his hips.

"So have you."

He shrugged. "It happens." Why did he seem so sad when he said that? As if he'd long since surrendered to some terrible reality about life that he was onto and I had yet to find out.

I ran my tongue along my lips, which were suddenly dry. He waved and moved off. "See you around."

"Sure."

I stood there as if I had just had a vision, staring at the spot in the hall where he'd been, thinking he might reappear, and wondering if I'd invented him. When Gina came in a few minutes later, I was still flushed and my head was ringing.

"I met your brother." I followed her into the kitchen.

In spite of the heat, she'd bicycled downtown to pick up some stuff from the deli for her mom. She's very athletic, tall and rangy and good-looking enough to be a model. "Oh, Josh." She set her package down on the counter.

"Where have you been hiding him?"

"What? Oh, hey, put the fangs back in, m'dear. He's not your type. He's an incurable flirt. Bad, Brie, I mean it. You'd just be one more notch on his gun. You know that trouble he got into at military school?"

"Well," I confessed, "I have heard something about it. I didn't want to ask you. I was just surprised to see him because I didn't know he was back."

"Oh, he's back all right. Well the trouble was over a girl. Some colonel's daughter, no less. Josh doesn't fool around with anybody but the best." She bit into a lush peach and offered me one. I went over to the sink to rinse it off.

"It was bad, Brie. Mom and Daddy are all torn up over it. We don't talk about it. Mom gets migraines. She's upstairs right now having one. She got it last night when Josh came home."

"Doesn't she like Josh?"

"Don't be silly, she loves him. She just worries over him so much, she gets migraines. He's been around, Brie. He's a hopeless womanizer. Has been since he was fifteen. Why do you think they sent him to military school? Why do you think they send him to Maine every summer?"

"Well, he seemed nice to me."

"Sure he seemed nice. He's adorable and I love him. As much as you love Kev. But he just can't help himself around women. I feel I gotta warn you."

I believed her. I thought no more about it or him. Why wouldn't I believe her? She was my best friend.

It was three whole weeks later, two weeks into the new school year, when I met him again. I was interviewing for a job on the *Close Call*, the school newspaper. I hadn't written for the paper up until then because, all through my freshman and sophomore years, I had been breaking my neck trying to make the swim team. But ever since eighth grade, I'd written poetry. Over the summer, I'd showed some of it to Kev.

We're pretty close that way. Most of the time, I can

confide in him when I wouldn't confide in Dad. Maybe it's because he's so much older, thirty-one years to my sixteen. Maybe it's because we became close after my mom left when I was two. My sister Ceil had been ten then and Kev, seventeen. But I became friends with Kevin rather than Ceil, who lorded it over me like older sisters sometimes do. And bossed me around. Kev was always gentle and protective.

Ceil left when she got old enough to go to college. She went to school on the West Coast, where Mom lived, and just never came back. That brought the three of us, me and Kev and Dad, even closer. Ceil is married now and has a toddler. I suppose I'll see her and Mom again someday, but I don't worry about it. They aren't part of my life anymore.

Anyway, when I showed Kev the poetry, he suggested I go out for the school paper in the fall. Armed with that much encouragement, I wrote some essays that Kev pronounced "comprehensive and insightful and sensitive."

It was cool, even for September, the day I met Josh again. I presented myself to David Sebring, first. He was the editor. He motioned me toward the assistant editor at the end of the office.

I didn't even know Josh was on the paper, much less an editor. I stood, numb and in shock, in front of his desk. It was piled high with papers and books and strewn with coffee cups and leftover hamburger. This time he was wearing neat chinos and a blue

crew-neck sweater. Was that why his eyes looked
even bluer than before? You can get that color in
your eyes from wearing contact lenses, I've heard. I
stood clutching the manila envelope in my hands,
feeling insipid and inadequate, and wishing I'd never
come. But it was too late to turn away. The blue eyes
were smiling up at me.

"You again."

I smiled back, managing to keep the tremor out of
my voice. "They told me you were the one I had to
see. I've got some stuff."

"Well." He shoved a coffee cup and some papers
aside and gestured to a chair. "Why don't you sit
down?"

Sit, yes, that was a wonderful idea. I bet he had
wonderful ideas like that all the time. I sat. He
reached across the desk for the envelope. I liked his
wrists. I fell in love with his wrists immediately. All
that dark hair on them. Slender yet strong. Oh no, I
thought, I'm feeling my hormones. Why didn't I
wear my good navy blazer instead of that stupid
sweater and jeans? Dress for success and all that. He
looked so sophisticated. I looked like what I was, a
stupid junior.

He shaved. Probably every day, I told myself.
Like Kev. So many seniors didn't yet. I shoved the
manila envelope across the desk. He took it, and I
went all weak inside. I could kill Gina, I told myself,
for not telling me her brother was assistant editor of
the paper.

"Brieanna McQuade," he read. "How's your dad doing with the *Journal?*"

"He's doing fine."

"His paper has been real generous with the scholarship fund for budding high-school journalists."

Why didn't I know anything about my father's scholarship fund? Here Josh was, in town only a couple of weeks, and he knew about it. If he thought me stupid, he didn't let on. He was reading one of my essays already. I waited.

"This is pretty good."

"It isn't funny," I said. "They do a lot of humor here."

"They do a lot of trash. Why do you want to write for us?"

"Well, my brother encouraged me to try."

"The priest?"

"What?"

"Your brother's a priest, isn't he? My mom goes to Saint Hedwig's. When he comes there on Sundays and gives his sermons, she goes wild. I think she wants to run away with him or something. She thinks he's great."

"He's at Saint Hedwig's all the time now. Father Roland had a heart attack, and Kev is filling in for him until he gets better."

"My mom told me he's a street priest in Newark. Works with the poor, she said."

"He is. He'd rather be in Newark than here. He doesn't like parish work. But he's doing it because he says he needs to grow as a priest and help all kinds of people."

"Does that mean you're religious? Because your brother's a priest?"

"I go to church. But I'm not one of those religious nuts."

"Good." He smiled. "I used to be Catholic. My whole family is. You know that. At military school, they made us go to services on Sunday. That's the only part of Chittendon I didn't like. Everything else I loved. I don't go to church anymore now that I'm home. My parents are ready to disown me. But, well, after all I'm eighteen now."

I just stared at him, wishing he would go on talking forever.

"Do you write poetry?"

How did he know that? Nobody knew that but Kev.

"There's a poetic quality to these essays."

"Oh. I couldn't figure out how you knew. Yes, I do, but I haven't shown my poems to anyone but Kev."

"Who?"

"My brother the priest. The one your mom wants to run off with." Oh, that was clever. Score one for me. I felt good. He smiled.

"Does it stifle your style, having a brother who's a priest? Do people expect you to be a goody-two-shoes?"

"I don't know, but I'm not."

"Good. Do you think you inherited your talent from your dad?"

"I didn't know I had any talent."

"You do. Look, I'm not fooling around. I'm just trying to bring you out of yourself a little. You're pretty uptight. Why are you so uptight? Do I make you nervous?"

I blushed. "Yeah."

"Why?"

"You just do."

He smiled again. I wished he wouldn't do that. Each time he flashed the strong white teeth, I went weak inside. Teeth are sexy, I thought. They could be one of the sexiest things about people. Why had I never had that particular revelation before?

He had gone back to his reading. I waited. Then, without looking up, he flung the next question at me. "Tell me, how does a girl who looks as attractive as you get to be able to write like this?"

I froze. I went hot, then cold. Surprised is what I was. And indignant. Because Gina had said he was so sophisticated with women and here he was using a variation of the oldest line in the world on me. I got up.

"What's the matter?"

"I thought you were being serious."

"Hey, wait a minute. Sit down. I was only testing you."

"Testing me? For what?"

"I'm sorry, please. Sit down. I was trying to see if
you'd come on to me. We're going to be working
closely on the paper, and...oh hell, this was all Sebring's idea, not mine. Lots of the girls have wanted
to sign on because they just want to fool around."

"You think an awful lot of yourself."

"It's not me, honest. It's Sebring. He wants to
make sure we're getting the serious types."

"And so? Have I passed your test?"

"I'm sorry. Yes."

"And what about you? What kind of a test did you
have to take?"

"Me?"

"Yes. I've heard about you."

"What have you heard?"

I said nothing, just stared at him stonily.

"Ladies' man? That what you heard? Did my sister tell you that?"

"I just heard it. Around."

"Yeah, well, do you always believe what you hear?"

"Not always."

"You shouldn't. If you hope to be a journalist. You
don't go on hearsay. You get the facts yourself. You're
a newspaperman's daughter. You should know better."

I felt reprimanded, as much as I'd ever been by
Dad or Kev. But more than that, I felt bad because
I'd misjudged him. "I do know better," I said. "And
I don't want to go on hearsay. Not about you. I'd
rather find out for myself."

His eyes grew soft and sad. "You have to be home right after school?"

"Well, if I don't get in by four o'clock, Alma is ready to send out the posse. But I told her I was trying out for the school paper today. So it's all right if I'm late. Why?"

"You have time to go for a little ride with me?"

"Where?"

"Someplace where you'll see what I'm all about. If you really want to know."

Chapter 2

It never occurred to me not to trust him. I felt, after the first fifteen minutes, as if I'd known him for ten years. He had an ease of manner, a ready smile, a gentleness about him that all added up to maturity. His body movements were unhurried and graceful. And although he was slender, his shoulders had a marvelous breadth beneath the oxford shirt. I noticed that more when he took off his sweater out in the school parking lot. We got into his silver gray sportscar and he rolled up the sleeves of his shirt and I could see the strength in his forearms and wrists. His hands I loved, of course. He had long fingers and neat nails. You can tell an awful lot from a man's hands. My dad has nice hands and so does Kev. I don't think I could stand a man with stubby hands. I watched him on the steering wheel as we pulled out of the lot.

"Where are we going?"

"Along the river on Route Three. Someplace special to me. I don't tell many people about it. Hardly any, as a matter of fact. But somehow I think you'd understand, and I want to share it with you."

That was enough for me at the moment. I settled into the seat of the sportscar. He put a tape into the tape deck. Surprisingly, it wasn't rock. No, I really wasn't surprised. I didn't expect him to like wild kid music. He was beyond that, I was sure of it, and that was what intrigued me about him. As Gina had said, he gave the impression of experience, all right. But somehow I didn't think it was the decadent kind she'd made it out to be. Somehow, I sensed a streak of sadness under his veneer of jokes and smiles.

He settled back in his seat too. "Tell me about yourself."

"I've told you so much already."

"You've been friends with my sister a long time."

"Since fourth grade."

"Your mom lives on the West Coast. And your dad has a girlfriend. Right?"

"Right. Amanda. She's lots younger than he is. She owns the Old Coach Restaurant in town."

"She used to be a model."

"What else did Gina tell you?"

"That's about it. She's pretty protective of you. Says I'd better stay clear of you or else. She'd be sore if she knew you were with me this afternoon."

"Will you tell her?"

"Probably not. Will you?"

I giggled. "No. Let's keep it a secret for now."

"Fine with me. Is your dad getting married to Amanda?"

"No, I don't think so. Not for a while anyway."

We were both silent for a bit, listening to the music. I felt as comfortable with his silences as I did with his chatter, I decided.

"I remember my mom telling me about the time, a few years ago, that she came home and found you two looking at an x-rated movie on the VCR. Boy, she was upset," he said.

"Your mom told you that?"

"She had to tell somebody. She couldn't go to Dad. He'd flip. I was at Chittendon then. She used to tell me lots of stuff that went on at home. Tell me about the x-rated movie. Where'd you get it?"

"I don't remember. Somebody's sister worked in a VCR store." I felt embarrassed talking about it now. It was something I would rather forget. Video tapes were just becoming popular, and Gina's parents had been one of the first people in Waltham to have a VCR. "We did it as a joke," I said.

"Some joke. My mom was all torn up about it. She didn't know what to do. Did she go to your dad about it?"

"No, she went to my brother after mass the very next day."

"Did he rat on you?"

"No. I asked him not to. Lots of times he doesn't

tell Dad things if he finds out I've done something wrong. He's pretty good about that."

"That's nice. To have somebody like that in your life, I mean. You realize how lucky you are? I wish I had somebody like him to go to, somebody close who was old enough to give advice and wasn't a parent."

He fell silent and I saw some shadow fall over him. "Well, it isn't all that peachy keen, I'll have you know. Kev wasn't exactly thrilled about it, either."

"What did he say?"

"Oh, he was all right. He could have been worse. He said the church was hung up on sex and sex wasn't the sin it's always made out to be."

"He said that?"

"Yeah. Kev's like that. He says he's a maverick priest. Lots of times he's in trouble with his superiors for some of the stuff he says and does. But they leave him alone, because he does so much good work. He said there were worse things than sex, like taking advantage of the poor and putting toxic wastes in the landfill and ruining peoples' lives with gossip."

"Right on."

"Yeah, sometimes Kev is really crazy. But he understands, that's the thing. Nothing shocks him. Oh, he was hurt when he found out about the tape. But we talked it out. He said he'd rather see people making love than killing each other. But that those movies weren't about real love. Or even real sex. He said anytime I had any questions about any of that, I should go to him."

"And have you?" His eyes were twinkling. I could tell he liked all this.

I shrugged. "Sometimes. Look, I don't tell a lot of the kids in school this stuff. Gina understands because she knows Kev. But the kids in school give me a hard time sometimes because my brother's a priest."

He nodded solemnly and got silent again. Why was he so interested in Kev, I wondered. I really never told anybody about the relationship I had with Kev. Most kids in school would make fun of it. But then, most of the kids in school were like Josh and had nobody to go to when they needed somebody they could trust.

"We're almost there," he said.

Ahead on the right was a sign. County Correctional Center. He pulled into the drive and guided the car slowly up the winding hill.

"Josh, this is a prison!"

Again, he flung me that knowing, easy smile. "Once you get inside and meet my friends, it won't make any difference."

A stab of panic went through me. "You have friends here?"

The smile stretched to its capacity. Why was it that whenever he smiled like that something hurt inside me? He pulled the car into the lot on top of the hill overlooking the river, cut the motor, and looked at me. "Yes. And they're the best kind of friends. They're animal, not human. You see, downstairs, in

that main building, the county runs a wildlife rehabil-
itation center. This is where the public comes to turn
in hurt or abandoned animals from the wild. There
aren't as many here as in the spring, but there are a
few I'd like you to meet."

"Why do you come here?"

He got out of the car and I got out on my side and
we fell into step on the gravel lot. "I volunteer my
time here whenever I'm home. Last spring, I was
home for a couple of weeks before I went to Maine,
and I took home a baby raccoon whose mother had
been killed. I had to feed him every four hours."

I stopped dead in my tracks, squinting at him in the
dappled September sunlight. "Gina never told me
that."

"There's lots of stuff Gina never told you about me.
That's what you're doing this afternoon. Finding out
for yourself. Remember? Come on, I want you to
meet Confucius and Clancy."

"Who are they?"

"Confucius is a great-horned owl and Clancy is a
white rat. They're downstairs in the main building.
There are others out in the yard, but we won't have
time for them today. You can come back and meet
them another day if you want."

He knew his way around, and his way was with
confidence and poise. I followed him up the cement
ramp to the entrance of the main building. Inside, he
presented himself before the window with a grin and

a wave to the prison guards in the round room behind
glass. They waved back, and I followed him down
the steps to the basement. We went into a little room
that seemed full of hutches, the kind kids have for pet
rabbits. Some had cardboard over the screen fronts.

"Now," Josh said, kneeling down in front of one of
the cardboard-covered hutches, "you are going to
meet a good friend of mine." And he unlocked the
door.

I heard movement inside, but at first, I saw nothing. Then two yellow round eyes stared out at us. It
was a huge owl, who looked extra large because his
feathers were all ruffled. Immediately upon sighting
us, he started making a clucking sound with his beak.

"Oh, Josh, he's beautiful! I've never seen a real
owl before!"

The owl just kept right on ruffling his feathers and
clucking.

"He's so enormous!"

"Come on, Confucius," Josh was saying, "nobody's
gonna hurt you. I just wanted you to meet Brieanna."

"Why's he making that noise?"

"We're invading his space. He's warning us to
keep away."

"I thought you were his friend."

He closed the door, secured the lock, and stood up.
"I can go just so far being his friend. He's not supposed to get attached to me. If he did, when he goes
back into the wild, he might see people and go for
them in friendship and it could be taken as an attack.

I shouldn't even be calling him by name. I gave him that name. I wasn't supposed to."

"I think that's awfully sad that you can't really be friends."

"Well, that's the way it is in life. Sometimes people can be only certain things to each other. That's the hardest thing I've ever had to learn or accept."

It was quiet in the room when he said this. And again I had the fleeting insight that he'd been through something bad enough to make those words ring true. "Hey, you see the incubators?"

He pointed them out to me in a corner of the room. "They're for baby rabbits and squirrels and raccoons. But the animals come in only in spring. Here, I want you to meet Clancy."

He took a cover off a large terrarium. Inside was a hollowed-out log and peering out of it was a white rat with red, beady eyes.

"He's pretty," I said.

"He was somebody's pet. Only they didn't want him anymore. We're trying to find a home for him."

"Is he alone in there?"

"No, there are others deep in the hollow of the log." He covered the terrarium. "Outside in the yard is the flight cage where Confucius will soon go. It's very long and high, and he'll exercise his flight muscles there. There are other wild things in the yard too, but we'd better leave them for another time. It's late, and they'll be wondering where you are at home."

I felt a warmth of tenderness because he thought of that.

"Why do you do all this, Josh?"

"I just like it." He shut off the light, and we went back up the stairs. "At Chittendon, I was studying biology and ecology. I want to be a wildlife specialist someday like Mr. Stephens, who runs this place for the county."

"But I thought you wanted to be a journalist."

He shrugged. "I can write articles about wildlife too. Only one thing." We walked through the foyer and out into the bright September sunlight. I realized how high we were on top of the hill, and looking around, I saw that the yard to the right of us was enclosed with a high wire fence that had rolls of barbed wire on top.

"I don't share this with the kids in school, Brie. You've probably noticed that I'm a loner. I haven't been around this town that much. And I don't feel close to too many people in school. You're the first one I've really made friends with."

"I heard you were out with Carla Beitel."

He grinned. "Yeah, I've been out with her. I'm not talking about casual dates. I'm talking about really being friends with people."

"But you must talk about something when you're on dates."

He grinned. "You want a list of all the girls I've been out with since I've been back in Waltham?"

"Have you dated many?"

"I haven't brought any of them here, if that tells you anything."

It did. I was moved.

"Does it bother you, this ladies'-man label I've got?"

"Let's just say it's intriguing."

"Would it keep you from going out with me?"

We were at the bottom of the cement ramp and the earth suddenly moved under me. At least that's how I felt. "I'm out with you now," I said lamely.

"I mean a real date."

"I...I don't know if my dad would like that, Josh. I don't even know if he'll like that I'm here with you today. He's pretty fussy about dating."

He wasn't stupid. "You mean he's heard about me, is that it? About Chittendon?"

I shrugged. "Everybody has."

"Wow." He plunged his hands into his pants pockets. He looked down, kicked a stone with his shoe, then took a deep breath, and looked around as if at the scenery. "Wow!" He was silent for a moment. Then, "That story has been exaggerated so much between Chittendon and here that I'm beginning to wish I'd done what they said I did, you know that? But look, how 'bout if I approach your dad and ask him."

"What would you say to him?"

"Leave that to me. Look, if he's the newspaperman

I've heard he is, he goes after the other side of the story, doesn't he? He doesn't accept hearsay. And he'll be fair. Won't he?"

"Yes, except you forgot one thing."

"What's that?"

"How do you know I want to go out with you again?"

He smiled. How could anybody smile when they had such sadness in their eyes. "What would make you say yes?"

"If you told me if you're wearing contact lenses, because I can't figure out how else your eyes can be so blue. They're even bluer than Kev's. And if you promised to bring me back to see the animals again."

"You have a deal. No, I'm not wearing contacts." Now he blushed. "That's just the color of my eyes. And yes, I'll bring you here again. But you gotta promise not to tell anybody in school."

"What makes you think some kids wouldn't under-stand?"

We were walking down the slope to the parking lot, and he paused and looked at me. "Do they under-stand about you and Kev?"

We got into the car and started down the hill. And we were both quiet for a while. I don't know what he was thinking, but I was realizing that Joshua Falcone had reached out in friendship to me that afternoon. And somehow, I sensed that I was very privileged.

Chapter 3

By the time we were back in Waltham, he had already proposed an idea for our first date. "How about the senior fall outing? It's supposed to be a camping trip. It's an overnighter, but your dad doesn't have to worry, it'll be well chaperoned. You like to camp?"

"I love it. I've been along on Kev's camping trips sometimes. He brings his inner city kids from Newark out here, and I sort of help him run things. I let him use my island."

"Your what?"

I giggled. "I have an island, didn't you know that? Devil's Own. You've heard of it, across from the state park."

"You own that island?"

"My grandmother left it to me last year when she died."

"Your own island? No kidding? Boy, and I thought

27

I was a spoiled kid with this sportscar."

"I'm not allowed to go out there alone. You have to take a boat from the state park across the river to get there. And Jim Varney, the ranger at the state park, is like a police dog for my dad. Anytime anybody wants to use the island, they have to sign in. I tried to rent a boat and go there once with some kids, and he even made me sign in."

"Still, it's a beautiful island," he said enviously. "So listen. The senior outing is supposed to be in the Poconos if we can get the money. If we can't, it'll be in the state park. Will you go with me? You could write a story about it for the *Close Call*."

"We could ask my dad if we could use my island if the Poconos don't work out," I said

The Poconos didn't work out. By the end of the week, I'd heard that; and by the end of the week, Josh had an appointment with my dad to ask if he could take me out.

"I'll ask him about the island," I said.

"I don't think you should. He'll think I'm asking you out for that reason. We can use the state park, Brie."

But I wanted to use my island. It had something to do with the fact that I was a junior going along on a senior camping trip and wanted to impress everybody. So I went along with Josh to my father's office and waited in the newsroom while Josh went in to talk to him. I'd ask him about the island afterward.

There are venetian blinds on the large window that faces the newsroom in my dad's office, but they were open, so I could see Josh sitting in a chair, see my father behind his rolltop desk, listening. They talked for almost an hour.

I sat in the newsroom attempting to read my history homework. I knew all the people in the newsroom, so I felt at home, but I still couldn't concentrate on my history. What could Josh possibly tell my dad that could whitewash the story about Chittendon?

To be sure, I didn't know the true story of what had happened at Chittendon. But I knew, from what Gina had told me about her family's reaction and from innuendos at school, that it had been bad. I sat there feeling pretty depressed, actually. My dad had mentioned nothing to me at breakfast or at dinner the night before about Josh's phone call. And I knew Josh had called him yesterday. I was convinced Dad would never let me go out with him.

Then the door of Dad's office opened and my father stood there, all six feet two of him, lanky and skinny, a distinguished-looking man of fifty-three with piercing brown eyes and a full head of graying hair. I loved my dad like nobody else in the world, but he certainly could scare me when he set out to do so.

He motioned me in. I left my books and went. Inside, he leaned back in his chair and regarded us both solemnly.

"You know what this is all about, Brie, I take it."

"Yes, Daddy."

"Josh here called me yesterday and asked to come in and see me, with the expressed intention of asking to take you out." He smiled. It was one of his dour smiles, with the corners of his mouth turned down. "I must say he took me by surprise with such old-fashioned manners."

Only two things had ever taken my dad by surprise in his thirty-two years of being a newspaperman—when my mom walked out on him and when his only son became a priest. But he weathered them both and came out on his feet. He's a survivor, my dad, if he's anything.

He's a decent, gentle man who has a long fuse, but you don't ever want to light it because his temper is fierce and he can hurt you with it. It's all part of his built-in sense of outrage and passion for justice. Above all, he hates lying and deceit.

Newspapering is his life's blood. He started out with practically nothing right after college and worked his way up to being editor of a Long Island paper, gaining a wide reputation as a fine newspaperman. When I was very small, he bought The *Journal*. It's a medium-sized daily that has won many journalism awards under his ownership. And because he has a competitor, The *Sentinal*, he sort of lives life on the edge. He says he likes it that way.

I know he wanted Kev to take over the paper someday. But he never talks about it anymore. He's accepted Kev's priesthood. He even takes a fierce pride in it now. When Kev first went off to the seminary, I think he wanted my sister Ceil to follow in his footsteps on the newspaper. But then she ran off.

Now there's only me. He doesn't say much about it, he doesn't push me, but I know he's watching to see if I'll fit the mold when I grow up.

"I told Josh," he was saying, "that I thought he was a little too old for you, Brie."

"Oh, Daddy!"

He scowled. "Two years is a big difference at your age. And you haven't dated that much."

I wished he hadn't said that. But he continued, ignoring my discomfort. "However, Josh came to me like a man and told me he knew he had more than that against him. He told me what happened at Chittendon. But he also said he's turning over a new leaf because he realizes how he's suffered for his behavior there."

He smiled again. I could tell he was about to have one of his indulgent moments. He plays all the roles in his life to the hilt, and being a daddy is one of the roles he loves best. He has a great sense of drama. And he likes it when people come to him with their problems and he can have an influence and make a difference in their lives. Josh had struck just the right note in approaching him like this.

"Josh told me he thinks he deserves a second chance. And we know about second chances in our family, don't we, Brie?"

"Yes, Daddy." He could be talking about his second chance at happiness with Amanda. Or he could be referring to Second Chance, the home for unwed mothers that Kev was opening in town for the church. My grandmother left Kev her Victorian home when she died. Kev was supposed to have the grand opening of Second Chance any day now.

My dad was looking at me. "Can't you say anything but 'yes Daddy'?"

"What else do you want me to say?" His direct manner sometimes caught me off guard, but it kept me on my toes. He had trained me to have certain qualities in life. Alertness, common sense, and honesty were the basics he expected. My father had his own laundry list of sins that were quite different from the ones Kev had for me. And if I committed any one of them, I heard about it.

"Well, for one thing, you could have told me you were going out for the school newspaper. That wouldn't exactly have thrown me into fits of despair." He was pleased. I ducked my head and shrugged.

"I didn't know if I'd make it, Daddy."

"Well, you have. And Josh tells me you'll be writing your first story on this outing. You know what I've told my daughter a person needs for the newspaper business, Josh?"

"No, sir. What?"

"Enthusiasm. Unflagging enthusiasm. Inquisitiveness. A sense of justice and fair play. A willingness to work hard. Some basic street smarts and a reasonable amount of craziness."

"Sounds good, sir," Josh said obligingly.

"Good? They're all necessary. Brie has just about all of those qualities. Kev is teaching her the street smarts. That's why I let her hang out with him so much. And she's got the craziness. Right, Brie? You inherited that from me, didn't you?"

He was showing off a little bit in front of Josh. "Yes, Daddy." I blushed.

He was right, though. I had all those qualities. I can't stand it when the little guy gets stepped on, and I hate it when somebody lies to me, although I've done a fair amount of lying in my time.

"Of course"—my father grew serious now—"I realize it didn't hurt your cause here today, Josh, to tell me Brie would be writing a story on this outing. Am I right?"

"I guess so, sir," Josh said honestly.

My father studied him for a moment. "I'm still giving my permission with reservations. I'm giving you your chance, Josh. I still think you're too old for Brie. She's a young sixteen. But I like the way you came to me today and laid everything out on the line. And I trust Brie. Don't disappoint me, either of you."

We both murmured that we wouldn't. Then it got silent for a moment, and I saw my chance. "Daddy, there's something else I have to ask you."

"Go ahead."

"The outing was supposed to be in the Poconos, but the senior class couldn't raise enough money. So now they are going to have it in the state park. But

I'd like to volunteer my island. Can I?"

He thought about that for a minute. He pulled out the bottom drawer of his desk, leaned back in his chair, and rested one foot on it. "Going to do a little showing off in front of the senior class? Is that it, Brie?"

I nodded yes, blushing.

"Well, all right. But you know I don't like big parties out there. Somebody trips over a log and breaks a leg, I'll be sued into next week."

"You said you had insurance, Daddy. You told Kev that when he brought his ghetto kids out there."

"Yeah, but I don't need the grief. All right, though. It is your island. I can't say no to you when I've said yes to Kev."

I got up. "Thanks a lot, Daddy." I went over to him and kissed the side of his face.

"Yeah." He waved me off. I could tell he was pleased, though. "Go on, both of you. I've got my editorial to write."

"You're going out with my brother on the senior camping trip? I knew it. I just knew it, McQuade. All this stuff about the school paper was just a front!"

Josh and I had decided it was time to tell Gina of our friendship. Now she stood next to me at the sinks in the girls' washroom at school, acting as if my date with Josh was a personal affront to our friendship.

"You said your father wouldn't even let you start dating steadily until you were a senior," she accused.

"Who said anything about getting heavy, Gi? It's one date."

"We promised each other we wouldn't go steady until then. That we'd stay friends. I know my brother. It'll be more than one date."

"Does it mean we can't be friends because I'm going on a stupid date with your brother?"

"I told you to watch out for him. You wouldn't listen." She was brushing her hair with vehemence.

"I don't get it, Gi. He's a perfect gentleman."

She stopped brushing. "I told you about Chittendon."

"Yes. But Josh told my dad about it. He said that getting kicked out of Chittendon was the worst thing that ever happened in his life and that he was going to turn over a new leaf."

"Oh, I'll bet he did!"

"I think your family is giving Josh a bum rap. You're not being fair to him. All he wants is a chance to prove himself."

"Well, he really got through to you, didn't he?"

"My dad wouldn't let me go out with him if he didn't think it would be all right, Gina. And what about me? We've been friends for so long. You know what kind of person I am. I'm not going to seduce your precious brother."

She just kept right on putting on lip gloss. "You're in over your head, Brieanna McQuade. And don't say I didn't warn you." She closed up the lip gloss and threw it in her pocketbook, snapped the purse shut, picked up her books, and turned to go.

"Gi?"

"What about the fact that my mom broke a golfing date to give you a body wave at our house on Saturday?"

"I'm sorry. I forgot. I'll call your mom and apologize."

"I'll bet you forgot. You know what makes me sore about this? The fact that you went behind my back with my brother."

I felt as if she'd slapped me. "Behind your back? I'm telling you about it."

"Yeah, well I still think the whole thing stinks."

"I don't believe all this, Gi, you know that? I don't believe that you can't trust your best friend and your brother on a date."

She knocked her pocketbook off the edge of the counter. It clattered to the floor, fell open, and things fell out. A pencil rolled, coins followed. A mirror smashed. We both knelt to retrieve the stuff at the same time. Our eyes met and I could see how betrayed she felt.

"You're in over your head, Brie," she said again. "Take my word for it, you won't be able to handle him."

We looked at each other, kneeling there on the floor, just for an instant before she turned away. And I realized that more than a mirror lay on the floor between us, irretrievable and shattered.

Chapter 4

Suppose I couldn't handle Josh? Gina's question spun around in my brain like my favorite jeans tumbling around in the dryer. I sat in the laundry room at home watching them through the glass door, tumbling with the rest of my clothes. Let's see, two heavy pairs of socks, down vest.

What was to handle? He hadn't even tried to put a hand where it didn't belong. And he'd had plenty of opportunity the day we went to the wildlife center.

Sweatshirt, camping utensils, sleeping bag, bug repellent. Suppose there was a spray you could use to repel boys? Would I use it on this camping trip with Josh? The answer was no. I didn't want to repel Josh. No, I didn't want to get into the sleeping bag with him, either. But that didn't mean I didn't want some of the preliminaries.

The idea of him even attempting some of the pre-

liminaries made me run cold all down my spine. But
I was sure he wouldn't. There was something about
him that was so...gentlemanly! Was that a corny
word?

Why had he picked me to go out with anyway?
Certainly he had his choice of older, prettier senior
girls. I stared at the spinning clothes in the dryer.
Suppose he really did want me along on this camping
trip only as a reporter. What would I do if he started
something, Gina wanted to know.

What would I do if he didn't?

The buzzer went off. The dryer stopped. The
clothes settled. I started to take them out, realizing I
was more worried about that than anything.

He didn't start anything. Twice he took my hand,
once when we were getting into his canoe at the state
park and once when we disembarked at my island.
Yet when he even did that or when he accidently
brushed against me the electricity between us was
almost visible. If he felt it too, he didn't let on. I
figured he was too experienced for that. But for me it
was as if the air, the water, the ground beneath us
were charged with electricity when I was near him.

It started out to be a good night. In the first place,
the kids all gave squeals of delight and grunts of admiration when our canoes reached my island. There
were murmurs of "Great, Brie," and guys saying to
Josh, "You sure know how to pick 'em." I think that
embarrassed Josh, because he was very quiet when

they said those things. I noticed he was very quiet around the other kids to begin with. They all respected him, but he wasn't really close to anybody.

Once on the island, of course, everyone got immediately busy. There were campsites to select, tents to erect, cooking utensils to get in order, work details to organize, and rules to set down by the teachers.

There were supposed to be seven teachers and twenty kids. Only four teachers showed, and for a while, it was pretty confusing. But then, out of the blue, Josh seemed to know what to do about setting up camp. After all, he'd been on bivouac enough at Chittendon. He didn't volunteer anything. He just started clearing an area and putting up a tent. I knew too, because I'd been on camping trips with Kev. And before you knew it Mr. DiSepio, who seemed to be the head honcho, put Josh in charge of overseeing the tents getting up.

Josh's was up already, and he was helping me with mine, which I was to share with Sharon Grunwich, a senior. We were doing pretty well on the tent, so Josh hopped around, helping everybody else.

I couldn't take my eyes off him.

Sharon and I were getting our sleeping bags and gear inside. "Boy, he's handsome," she said. "You can tell he's been away at school. He's light years beyond these other guys. I can't believe he got kicked out of that place. What'd he do?"

"I don't know," I lied. All I did know was that it had to do with a girl, but I wasn't going to tell her that. A couple of the senior girls came up to me that night and said nice things about Josh.

"You're a pretty sly one, McQuade," Andrea Dennison said. "And here we thought you were a mousy little junior."

I ignored that. I wasn't going to let anybody ruin the night for me. The air was charged with possibilities, the food never tasted so good, there was a mystical quality to the campfire. After supper, the kids started to pair off and move away.

"Not too far, kids," DiSepio called. "We want you within calling distance."

It got dark. Josh got caught up in a conversation with DiSepio, who'd once been in the army and felt they had a lot in common. I was bored with the talk but happy to be near Josh, who was very considerate and attentive, giving me a sweatshirt, getting me coffee, and trying to include me in the conversation.

About ten o'clock, DiSepio looked up at the sky. "Looks like rain."

"Yeah, you ought to start circulating and pick up notes for your story, Brie," Josh said.

Some kids were already settled in tents—not necessarily their own. It was drizzling and everyone was starting to take cover. Josh hurriedly gave me his parka and said he'd be in his tent and that he'd find me later. The teachers would make a head count at midnight. I found Vera Holt and Christine Corcio in a tent with Evan Hilary and Barry Buetell, their respective boyfriends.

"Aw, come off it. The whole dumb school knows your brother is a priest."

"I never tried to hide it."

"Yeah, but a cute kid like you. It's a shame."

I felt myself getting hot in the face, and I was about to tell him off and to devil with the interview when Christine Corcio intervened. "Why don't you leave her alone and let her do her story, Barry. Maybe you're wasted, but the rest of us want to cooperate."

The others answered my questions. When I got to Buetell, he offered me another beer. "I had one already," I said.

"Oh, I forgot. Goody-two-shoes doesn't drink."

I took the beer, opened it, and took a swig. He grinned. "Proceed with your questions," he said.

It rained harder, and even though I got everything I needed from them, I hung around the tent for a while. I think it was a subconscious thing to show them I could drink their beer even though my brother was a priest. They were all taking note of it, even the girls. I caught them surreptitiously exchanging glances as I accepted the third can.

By the fourth, I wasn't sure I could get up. I felt very loose limbed and giggly and flushed in the face. The downpour had stopped by my fourth beer. Thank heaven for that. I don't know how many I could have taken to prove that my priest brother didn't cramp my style. When I got up to go, my head was swimming, my eyes were not quite focused, and I became confused making my way back to my tent.

There were other kids I had to interview, but I could
do that tomorrow, I decided. Right now, I felt nau-
seous inside and too lightheaded for my own good. I
wanted to find Josh.

I didn't get the full picture of what was happening
right off. How could I? I couldn't have focused on
the full picture. There seemed to be an awful lot of
confusion. The teachers, Mullin, Cosgrove, DiSepio
and Messerole, couldn't seem to handle things.
Twenty kids were scattered around and it was dark
and the teachers seemed to be all over the place suddenly, trying to round them up.

I almost bumped into Josh. "What's going on?"

"Where the hell've you been?"

"Wha...I was over there...I—"

"You've been drinking too? Like all the others?"

I looked up at him dumbly. He held a large flash-
light, and in the background, it seemed all I saw were
flashlights and lanterns bobbing around. I wished
they wouldn't bob around so. "What others? What's
everybody so crazy for?" I giggled and swayed.

"Brie, you're drunk!"

"I am not," I said indignantly.

"I should never have left you alone. There's been
drinking going on like crazy here tonight. The kids
smuggled beer in. The teachers found out, and
everything's gonna hit the fan in a few minutes. Did
you get your interviews?"

Again I giggled. "Oh, Josh, you look just like Kev when he gets sore."

"Come on over here where they can't see you." And he pulled me into the shadows.

"Oh. Don't walk so fast. You look just like Kev. And he's a priest. Where are you taking me?"

"Just pray the teachers stay busy for a while rounding up the kids. Here." He'd poured water into a wooden bucket and handed me a washrag that had been dipped into it. "Put this on your face."

I took it. "Oh, it's cold."

"Do it again," he ordered.

"I'm all right. Really."

"Do it *again*. You're *not* all right." Then he pushed me to kneel on the ground and knelt next to me and dipped the washrag in the cold water again. I put it on my face. "Oh, Josh, I don't feel so good."

"Wha'd ya go drinking all that beer for?"

"I don't know."

"Well, you're in a mess now. Come on, keep rinsing your face. Bend over and splash the water on it. Go ahead."

I did as he told me. Several times. The cold water shocked me at first, but it felt good. He was in the background now. He came back with a cup of coffee. "Here, drink this."

I sat on a log and sipped it. "Oh, it's black. I like it with cream."

"Just drink it. Don't give me an argument."

"Don't talk to me like that." I started to cry.

"I'd like to spank you." He suddenly sounded like my father. "We promised your dad everything would be okay and now look at you. What's gotten into you anyway? Why'd you drink the beer? You can't drink. Anybody can see that. Who gave it to you?"

"If you don't stop, I won't answer one question. You're not my father."

"Yeah, but when your dad finds out about this you'll be answering, all right. So you might as well tell me. Why did you do it?"

I sipped the dark sweet brew. My head felt better since the cold water treatment, but my stomach was giving me grief now. "They were on me, because my brother is a priest."

"Wonderful," he said. "Now they know you're just as much of a slob as the rest of them."

"Joshua!" I did cry then. I couldn't help it. The tears started coming fast and furious.

"Stop it," he whispered fiercely.

I couldn't. He took out a handkerchief and wiped my face. "I'm sorry. I shouldn't have said it. You're not like the rest of them. You're a sweet, decent kid, and I shouldn't have brought you here tonight. It's my fault."

"I'm not a kid. I can take care of myself."

"Well, you're not doing such a great job of it, are you?"

"I just couldn't stand them sneering at me because my brother's a priest."

"Well you're gonna have to toughen up about that. Not let them get to you."

"I goofed, didn't I. I didn't get my interviews done."

"You can get the rest tomorrow. Look, why don't you let me get this bucket to your tent? Take your coffee and lay low in there a while and keep splashing water on your face. They're heading back this way. It'll be a while before you're missed. Try to get yourself in order."

"All right," I agreed meekly.

I did as he suggested. I stayed in my tent drinking my coffee and dipping the washcloth into the cold water and applying it to my face. Outside, it was panic time. It sounded something like parents trying to round up third-graders at the zoo. The grown-ups were opening tent flaps to shrieks and giggles. There were stern reprimands and sharp orders. Through the slit in my tent flap, I could see them herding kids into the circumference of the firelight.

One or two kids had already passed out. It was a little after midnight.

"Where's Innocenzi?" I heard Miss Cosgrove ask.

"In the bushes being sick."

"Go get him. Where's Rosen?"

"I think he's out cold in his tent."

"Well get him up! I want him out here now," Cosgrove ordered. "You there, Falcone, you been drinking?"

"No, ma'am."

"You're the one who went to military school, right?"

"Yes, ma'am."

"Okay, you stay here and keep these kids in order while we flush the others out."

No sooner had I heard that than my tent flap was opened. I glanced up, startled, to see Mr. DiSepio leaning in to look at me. "You alone in there, McQuade?"

"Yes, sir."

"Come on out here. Now."

I stumbled out to stand in front of him. "You been drinking?"

"No, sir."

"You're lying, McQuade. How old are you? Sixteen? You're only a junior, aren't you?"

I stared up at him, petrified. I'd had him sometimes for math when my regular teacher was sick last year. I knew how tough he was. He squinted down at me in disgust. "You've been drinking. You lied."

"No, sir, I—"

"Go on out there with the rest of them. Let's see if you can walk, McQuade." We walked in the direction of the campfire. "I've got one more," he announced. "The owner of this island. The one whose father is a prominent newspaperman in town. And whose brother is a priest."

I felt everything sort of turn around inside my stomach. Clearly, I was finished.

Mr. DiSepio made a speech once everyone was assembled. They'd found out about the beer, he said, but somebody suggested there were drugs around. So everybody was to turn out the pockets of their clothing while the other teachers searched the tents.

"That's against our constitutional rights," somebody yelled.

"Quiet!" DiSepio ordered. "You've got no constitutional rights here tonight. You gave them up, as far as I'm concerned, when you brought the beer in."

Then DiSepio enlisted Josh to stand guard over the kids around the campfire to keep them from wandering off, while he and two sober senior girls started down the line. Everybody had to turn out pockets. As they came toward us, I saw Buetell, out of the corner of my eye, edging his way over to Josh, who was standing next to me. I thought he wanted to tell Josh something. But what happened, instead, was like a crazy slow-motion underwater ballet.

Buetell came right up behind Josh. "Do me a favor, huh, good buddy?" And I heard his low laugh. "They'll never search you, soldier boy."

"What the hell...." Josh turned, and it was like a good play in a football game with Buetell shoving something into his hands. Then Buetell was gone, back to his place in line before he was missed.

I heard Josh groan and curse softly.

"Josh?"

"I've got to get rid of this stuff!"

I looked down at what he held in his hands. A

plastic bag full of junk. White stuff and pills, lots of
them.

"Drugs, Brie," he whispered. "Coke, pills, everything."

To the left of us, DiSepio and the two senior girls
were working their way down the line. Josh
groaned. Then DiSepio yelled, "You there, Falcone?"

"Yes, sir."

"Come on over here, I need your help."

"Yes, sir." He looked at me, wild-eyed. I had
never seen such sheer terror in anybody's eyes in my
life. And I knew what he was thinking. I just got
kicked out of one school, now this.

"Give them to me," I whispered.

He just looked at me, dazed.

"I said give them to me! I'll hide them. I know
where."

"No, I can't let you."

I pulled the bag from his grasp and ran off with it
into the night, into the dark of my island that I knew
so well. I turned only once to see Josh staring after
me, then he went over to DiSepio.

I worked fast. My head cleared. First, I had to orient myself. The sound receded in the background as
I made my way further into the dark. Where was that
tree, the one with the hollow in the trunk? Up ahead,
to the left a little. I almost tripped, but caught myself
and stumbled along the familiar path. I found the

tree and stuffed the bag into the hollow. Then I held my pounding head and threw up.

"Where you been, McQuade?" DiSepio was glaring at me across the circle of firelight. "Well? Where'd you wander off to without permission?"

"I had to throw up."

He scowled. "Put her down on the list," he said. Cosgrove had a clipboard in her hand and was marking down names.

"What's that for?" I asked.

"It's a drunk list," DiSepio said. "It goes to the principal. Most likely, it'll go down on your permanent record. Your parents will receive a call."

I took my place back in line feeling more cold and sick and dismal than ever before. But across the circle of firelight, I caught Buetell watching me with the closest thing to admiration he could manage under the circumstances.

Chapter 5

The lights were out in my house when we pulled into the driveway. They started going on, one by one, right after that. First, the light in my father's bedroom upstairs. Then in the living room and kitchen. Josh and I just sat there watching.

"I'm sorry how this turned out, Brie."

"I'm the one to say I'm sorry to you."

"It doesn't matter. The whole night's been a nightmare."

It had been. The teachers had decided to ferry twenty kids back across the river in the dark rather than police them through the night. The few seniors besides Josh who hadn't been drinking had been parceled out in the canoes with the kids and delegated, after we got back to the state park, to take them home. A lot of camping gear had been left on the island, most of it to be picked up later by parents.

Josh and I had taken three kids home.

"There were drugs all over the place," Josh said now. "The island was crawling with them."

"Did anybody get caught?"

"No, I don't think so. I think it was all in that one bag. What did you do with it?"

"I stuffed it in the hollow of a tree."

"You're pretty terrific, you know that? Any other girl would have panicked."

"Yeah, well I'm not every other girl."

"I tell you, I was scared, Brie. I don't need to be kicked out of another school. You did me a big favor. I owe you."

"You helped me get myself together tonight, didn't you?"

He leaned back in the seat and closed his eyes. "Boy, I don't need to be kicked out of another school!"

We were both silent. The specter of Chittendon lay between us.

"Josh? You never did tell me what happened at Chittendon. I know you told my dad. But you never told me. The kids tonight were bugging me about it."

"What did you say?"

"That it was none of their business."

"You want to know though, don't you?"

I shrugged. "It does bother me some. Not what you did but that you won't tell me."

He shifted his position, half facing me. "I'm sorry. I do owe you an explanation. I had this romance with

Colonel Sequist's daughter."

"Romance?"

"Well, you could call it that."

"You mean you had sex with her?"

"Hey, come on."

"Did you?"

He smiled and brushed my hair back from my face. "Yeah. She was pretty advanced for her age. I didn't really seduce her, Brie. You can believe that or not. She kept after me. I know how egotistical that sounds, but she did. She was attending a nearby high school, and she lived at home. I was at the colonel's house a lot, because he had this collection of botany books I was cataloging for him. I got extra credit for that."

"Did you get extra credit for carrying on with his daughter?"

"Stop it. Don't be sore. That was all before I knew you. You think I haven't suffered enough for that? Hey, I liked the colonel. And he trusted me. And when he found out, he was sore as anything. And disappointed in me. And her. It was the worst thing I ever did in my life, and I regret it every day. I miss Chittendon something fierce. I wanted to graduate from that place."

I said nothing.

"So, I've told you now. You gonna hold it against me?"

"No."

He grinned. "I've been celibate ever since."

"What?"

"You know, like a priest. Like your brother. This reputation I have follows me around. I'm trying to get rid of it. I almost ruined myself, so I've vowed to be celibate."

"Is that what you told my dad?"

"Yes. Look, I'll call you tomorrow morning when you're feeling better, and you can tell me where you hid the stuff. I'll have to go get it in my boat and ditch it in the water. We'd better go inside now. We gotta face your father sooner or later."

My father was wearing his designer robe when he came to the door. The one Amanda had given him last Christmas. Maroon velour. He was wearing it over his pajamas.

We followed him into the center hall. I dumped my camping gear on the floor. Beyond, in the amber light of the living room, I saw Amanda set down the phone. "Another call, Jim. Another parent. I said you'd get back to them tomorrow. Oh, you two! We were so worried!"

I could see how worried they'd been. She was wearing an ice blue negligee and wrap with ivory lace trim. Amanda was only thirty-four. She had real blond hair, a slim figure, and still looked like a model. Never before had I seen her in our house in anything but street clothes. But then, they hadn't been expecting us home tonight. And Alma always spent Friday night with her family across town.

"What happened?" my father asked.

"Everything's okay, Dad."

"Sure. For the last hour, I've been getting phone calls from every parent in town telling me about the orgy the senior outing turned into. And you stand here telling me everything is fine?"

"It wasn't an orgy, Mr. McQuade," Josh said.

My father turned to look at him. "I trusted you to take out my daughter."

"Yes, sir. I'm sorry about all this. Some kids smuggled in beer and got drunk."

"Were you drinking, Josh?"

"He wasn't, Daddy," I said. "He was the one the teachers depended on to help."

"You'll get your chance to talk." My father's brown eyes were black with emotion. "What about you. Were you drinking?"

"I had a couple of beers, Daddy."

The eyes got blacker. He wheeled around and gestured that we should follow him into the living room.

More than anything in the world, I craved my father's approval. I had long since learned how adept he was at dispensing and withholding it as he saw fit. In the living room, he settled in a chair and indicated that we were to sit.

"I've got coffee," Amanda said. "You both must be chilled. And sandwiches. They'll be ready in a minute."

Did they know how cozy they looked in their at-

home outfits? Amanda went floating back into the
kitchen trailing her perfume and ice blue wrap, looking sophisticated and elegant. I felt a stab of resentment at finding them like this. But apparently they
were oblivious to the whole situation. Oh, I knew
they'd been sleeping together. But it was something
that I suspected went on only at her place. Somehow,
I felt that my father had broken some unspoken
agreement he had with me, bringing her into our
house like this. It hurt me something awful.

He looked at us. No one could be more tender and
charming than he when he chose to be. And no one's
anger was more devastating. I knew he'd question us
first, get the details, hear us out. I also knew that his
wrath, if it came, would be a creative wrath, tailored
to the offender, designed to find one's weak spot and
tear right into it.

"So you weren't drinking, Josh?"
"No, sir."
Amanda came back in with coffee and sandwiches,
and Dad gestured that we should eat. We ate and
drank some coffee. My father just puffed his pipe and
watched us. Then, almost on signal, Amanda announced she was going to bed.

"I'm in the spare room, Brie, if you want me for
anything."

Yeah, right. Sure. What does she think, I'm dumb
or something? She left and then Dad started in with
the inquiry, the questions coming rapid fire with his

usual piercing ability to learn the truth.

Were all the kids drinking? How many teachers were there? How many were supposed to have chaperoned? Were they doing their job or goofing off? Were the kids drinking anything else but beer? Drugs? Were there any drugs around?

"Oh, no, sir," Josh said. "No drugs." I was surprised at how effortlessly he lied. I couldn't look at him. I wasn't a good liar. Oh, I could manage to get away with it now and then with Dad. But Kevin always saw through me.

"Do you realize I'm going to have to write an editorial about this?" He turned to me. "Who do I come down on? And how do I do it when my own daughter was one of the offenders?"

"I'm sorry, Daddy," I said.

"Where were you when she was drinking, Josh?"

"I was talking. Brie was in the tents. Getting her interview. I'm sorry, Mr. McQuade, I didn't know...."

Dad nodded. "You were drinking on the job?" He was incredulous. "I'd fire you in a minute for that. No newspaper union contract could protect you either. You know that?"

I said nothing. I could see how disappointed he was.

"Were you drunk?"

"No," I lied.

He nodded, puffing his pipe. "I think you better go to bed now. We'll talk about it in the morning."

I got up. "Daddy, you're not gonna blame Josh. He wasn't even with me when I had the beer."

"No, Brie, I'm going to hold you completely responsible for your own actions."

He was sore. As sore as anything.

"See ya, Josh," I said.

"Yeah, Brie."

"Good night, Daddy."

Chapter 6

It was the phone that woke me the next morning, ringing through the house. I opened my eyes to streaming sun coming in through the organdy curtains at my window. My head hurt something awful and my mouth was parched and I felt stiff all over as I got out of bed and made my way to the bathroom in the hall. I showered, holding my head under the water, trying to make things clear. It helped a little. Then I got dressed and went downstairs.

My dad was alone at the dining room table, reading his paper. The *New York Times* and his paper's rival, The *Sentinal*, were on the table next to him. He reads both every morning. Usually on Saturday, I'll come downstairs and find a guest at the breakfast table. All kinds of people drop in on weekends. Sometimes, one of his reporters or editors will stop by. Other times just a plain citizen, and Daddy will invite that person to sit down and eat. One morning, I came down and found the police chief at our breakfast table.

Alma doesn't usually come back from her day off with her family until late Saturday, but the table was set for three. My dad had done that. He can sometimes make out very well with domestic things when Alma isn't around. It was very touching to see him seated there all alone, the table perfectly set, reading.

"Good morning, Daddy." I slipped into my place.

"Morning." He was reading. I poured myself some coffee. I was dying for coffee. He raised his eyebrows. "I made a batch of pancakes. They're in the toaster oven. Go get them."

My dad's pancakes were pretty good. He was an expert at them. I filled up my plate in the kitchen and came back and ate them. He kept reading. Neither of us spoke.

When I got finished, he leaned back in his chair. "I got a phone call this morning from Mr. Randolph, Brie. You're down on a drunk list."

There was a scowl of concern on his forehead. The brown eyes were full of that same concern. And hurt.

My temples throbbed.

"Were you drunk?"

I shrugged. "I don't know, Daddy."

"You don't know?"

"I didn't feel so good last night."

"How do you feel now?"

"I've got a headache and I feel crummy."

"How many beers did you have?"

"Four." I raised my eyes tentatively to look at him.

"You lied to me last night about being drunk. Why?"

"I was scared, Daddy."

He got up and walked casually into the kitchen to the Lazy Susan on the counter, took something from it, then went to the fridge and came back with some tomato juice. He poured the juice into a glass, took out two aspirin, and put them down on the table and went and sat down. He sipped his coffee. I took the aspirin and drank the juice.

"When was the last time I laid a hand on you, Brie?" he said quietly.

"You never have, Daddy."

"Then why did you lie to me? What are you afraid of?"

He had to ask? His brown eyes, looking at me full of disappointment—that's what I was afraid of. Of the hurt in his voice. Of facing him like I had to do now. I loved him so much. I wanted to be everything he wanted and I couldn't. Didn't he know that? I'd heard from Kev that there were people in his newsroom who felt that way about him, who knew what a special person he was and craved his approval.

I looked at him bleakly.

"You know how I hate lying. You *know* that." He sighed, shook his head. "The beer is something else. That goes on your permanent record. That's bad enough! I'm going to have to go and see Randolph, and try to get your name off the damned drunk list. How bad were you?"

"I wasn't that bad, Daddy. Just a little confused. By the time Mr. DiSepio caught up with me I was all right. Josh made me wash my face in water and gave me coffee. I don't think I was really *drunk*, Daddy, but I was drinking."

"You weren't drunk when you came in last night. I'd know if you were. So your name doesn't deserve to be on that list. Still, you'll take whatever punishment the school metes out. I'm staying out of that. But I will get your name off the list. And I'll have to say, in my editorial, that my own daughter was involved."

I nodded.

"Now why did you do it? The beer, I mean."

Could I tell him? I considered for a moment, decided to try. "I did it to prove I'm a regular person even though my brother's a priest."

"I see. Kids giving you a rough time, is that it?"

"Sometimes they do."

He was silent for a while. He poured himself another cup of coffee, stirred in the sugar quietly. I watched his every move. He's graceful for such a tall man, graceful as a cat, and as wary.

"Sooner or later in life, you're going to have to ask yourself to what lengths you'll go to prove you're still a regular person even though your brother's a priest. You know that, don't you?"

"I know it now, Daddy."

He nodded.

"Look, let's get this over with before Amanda comes down. You're grounded for two weeks. That's for lying to me more than for the beer, although it's for the beer too. You are expressly forbidden to go to the island under any circumstances for two weeks. At the end of two weeks, I'll decide if I want you to see the Falcone boy again."

"But Daddy, it wasn't Josh's fault!" Tears came to my eyes.

"I didn't say it was. I'm going back to my initial reaction, which was that I think he's too old and experienced for you. You should be hanging out with sixteen-year-olds. Not eighteen-year-olds."

"But Josh is decent, Daddy, he really is. He kept his promises to you."

"Brie, all I know is you were drinking. And you lied to me. I'm not saying it's his fault. But I am reserving judgment on whether you can see him again. I need time. Now don't give me any arguments. I think I let you off pretty easy."

I didn't have time to argue. Amanda came sweeping into the room then. "Good morning, oh it *is* such a lovely morning after the storm last night." She looked good in her new fall tweed suit and cashmere sweater—all beige and brown and gold. Real gold bracelets dangled from her wrists and earrings from her ears. My father had given them to her. She went and kissed the side of his face.

"I'm late. I can't linger, Jim, I hope you don't

mind. I've got oodles of people coming to the restaurant to see me about things. I'll just have juice and
coffee. Brie, why don't you stop by later? I'll give
you some lunch. Is that all right, Jim?"

"Brie is grounded, but she can have lunch with
you, yes."

"Brie?" She looked at me, but I didn't answer.

"You can at least be polite," my father said icily.

"I have to go to the library this morning," I said,
"but okay, I'll have lunch with you."

"Good."

"Can I go over to Second Chance and see Kev after
lunch, Daddy?"

"I wish you would." He sighed. "I wish you'd
have a nice long talk with Kev. As a matter of fact, I
hope you intend to tell him what happened last night,
because I don't want to be the one to tell our smiling
Irish priest that his little sister was cited for drinking."

Josh called before I left. Luckily, he reached me on
my phone in my room. I gave him directions to the
hollowed-out tree, as best as I could. Then there was
a momentary silence.

"Your father say anything to you this morning?" he
asked.

"Randolph called and told him I was on a drunk
list, and so Dad grounded me for two weeks. We
won't be able to see each other."

"We can, in school. Your dad's pretty decent, Brie.

I know he was hurt last night, but he was decent to me anyway."

"What do you think Randolph will do to us?"

"I don't know, but he's been calling every parent of every kid who was there. Look, I gotta run. I want to get over to the island before the parents get there to retrieve the camping gear. Where will you be today if I need you?"

"I'll be at Second Chance after lunch. Lunchtime I'll be at Amanda's restaurant. I wish I could go with you, Josh."

"So do I. But you'd better be good for a while. Hey, I'll call you."

It was a bright copper-penny morning. I put on my hooded sweatshirt and threw some books into my backpack and set off on my bike for the library. On the way, I passed Gina and Josh's house. His car wasn't in the driveway. The shade at Gina's bedroom window was still down. I felt the pain of our argument, like a finger I'd cut yesterday, mingling with the new-found warmth of Josh's friendship.

Had I traded off one friend for another? Did it have to be that way? A sense of loss flooded me. I needed Gina now. We'd been as close as sisters, trading clothes, cutting each other's hair, commiserating over our looks or celebrating them. We'd borrowed money from each other, cried together at movies. What right did she have to get mad at me for going out with her brother?

I spent an hour at the library, then went to Amanda's restaurant. My head felt better, riding in the morning air, and by the time I got there, I was hungry.

Her accountant was with her, so she didn't have a lot of time for me, but the cook got me some gourmet soup and a croissant sandwich. Finally, she had a few minutes to sit down with me and have some tea.

She smiled. "Your dad okay?"

"Uh huh."

"He seemed all right last night. But when I came down this morning, you two seemed at odds."

"Randolph, the principal, called him. I'm on a drunk list at school."

"Oh no! Oh, that's terrible."

"Daddy's pretty upset. He says he's gonna try to get my name off the list. And now he says he has to write an editorial about it. And I'm grounded for two weeks, and I don't know if he's gonna let me go out with Josh again."

She nodded. She didn't deliver any lectures, at least. Lots of times, she just listens when I need somebody to listen. I guess she knows I've got enough people telling me what to do between Dad and Kevin.

I don't resent her or the place she occupies in my father's life. She's the only serious relationship he's had since Mom left when I was two. I thought it was kind of foxy of old Dad to find somebody as young and pretty as she is. Last night had just shocked me, her being in the house in her nightclothes, that's all.

"Josh is nice," she said. "He looks decent. And he's so handsome."

"He was kicked out of Chittendon. You know that."

"We all make mistakes in life, Brie. I made a few when I was young. You'll have to be good for a while. Let your father get over this. I'll put in a good word for you, if you want, about Josh."

She was looking at me speculatively. What was she saying? That I should accept last night and try to understand? Whatever she was saying, I sure could use any help she could give. I know how much influence she has with my dad, and she's still young enough to identify with how it was when she was my age. I can say that much for her.

"Thanks Amanda," I said. "I can use whatever help I can get."

Chapter 7

Our smiling Irish priest, as Dad called him, was in the backyard when I came around the corner on my bike. The whole backyard of the big old Victorian house that my grandmother used to own was dug up. Something to do with the plumbing system. Kev had to have all kinds of renovations done to the house to comply with the housing authority rulings for multiple dwellings. Within a week, three unwed mothers were supposed to move in. But before that, there would be a ribbon-cutting ceremony with church officials and social workers and the press.

I'd helped Nastasha, the director, pick out the curtains and bedspreads for the girls' rooms. She had been an unwed mother herself. She was now studying for her doctorate, and Kev hired her to live in and run the place, because he figured the girls would identify with her.

I parked my bike in the side yard of the house. Through the bushes, I could see Kev standing in jeans and T-shirt, talking with the workers. He needed a shave. He looked tired too.

Since he'd taken over duties at St. Hedwig's for Father Roland, he was running himself ragged, doing it all—sick calls, morning mass, baptisms, weddings, confessions, meetings. He doesn't really like parish work. But he thought he needed a taste of it. He felt obligated to Father Roland, who'd helped him get Second Chance established in town. And at least at St. Hedwig's, he could be near Second Chance instead of running in from Newark all the time.

He prefers his real job, which is being a street priest in Newark. That's his ministry, he says. His whole life is dedicated to helping the poor. It's all he wants. And he does it with such unfailing humor and hope, it could break your heart.

We were close, like I'd told Josh. Ever since I was a little kid, we'd discussed things. Oh, sometimes we fought like brother and sister. But he's chased off my demons, listened to me, seen the blackness in my soul, and loved me anyway.

I'm not the only one who feels that way about him. Everybody who comes in contact with him knows what a good priest he is. Like now, out there in the yard in jeans and T-shirt with the workmen. He believes that God is in the street and the workplace. And he takes off his priest clothes and gets right in there with the people. He doesn't shove religion down their throats either. He's helped lots of people who aren't even Catholic. He knows about things like housing and medical care and feeding the hungry. People come to him for help who don't even go to church.

Me? I'm lucky to have him as my brother. There's a real compulsion in the way I go to him when I'm bothered. It never seems to surprise him, but it surprises me. Because sometimes he gives me answers I don't like and I go away mad. But I always go back again. There's something about his lopsided grin that gets me. Or maybe I'm drawn by the hard kernel of truth behind the blue eyes. By the light in those eyes and whatever is behind it.

Sometimes I'm snotty to him, but he forgives me. My snottiness is a defense against his attacks on my soul. He wants my soul. That's okay, it's his business to want my soul.

It's my business to hold on to it.

But I respect him and he knows that. So I allow him to go after me, to tease me into seeing my faults. He always knows when to stop. He knows my limits and my needs.

I love him, but I'm afraid of him too. Because he's got this power. It's there, I can see it and feel it. Sometimes I'm drawn to it like a moth to a flame. Sometimes I dance around it, I flirt with it, I elude it. It's a sort of game between us, but it's an honest game and each of us knows the rules.

I can lie to Dad and get away with it. But not to

Kev. He knows sin. Something inside him, old as the ages, recognizes it. And when he does, when he sees the sin inside me, I'm a little kid again. On top of the ladder. That's when I learned how it was always going to be with me and Kev. When I was about five years old.

He was home from the seminary for Christmas, and he was decorating the tree. I had a thing for Christmas tree balls. They were so beautiful that I wanted to grab them, hold them, possess them. Only, the night before, when he'd opened boxes of balls, I'd grabbed one and run off with it and held it too tightly in my hand. I'd crushed it and cut my hand. I still had the bandage on.

While Kev was decorating the tree, I kept reaching for the balls and taking them off the branches, in spite of his repeated requests for me to stop. There was a stepladder next to the tree. It wasn't very high, one of those five-or six-step things. I remember grabbing a ball from the tree and running off with it. I remember Kevin calling my name sharply. Then he came after me and picked me up and set me on top of the stepladder and told me to sit there while he continued his tree-trimming. At first I was fascinated, then frightened, then helpless.

The phone rang, and he went into the hall to answer it. Moments later, my father wandered in.

"What are you doing up there?" he asked.

"Kev put me here."

"Why?"

I told him why. He stood there, eye level with me, lighting his pipe, and considering the situation. "When Kevin is ready he'll take you down," he said. He stayed there in the room until Kevin came back, probably to make sure I didn't fall, but he wouldn't lift me down, in spite of my pleadings. Then, as soon as Kev walked into the room, he left.

Once when I was older, I asked Dad why he hadn't rescued me from the ladder that day.

"There are some places in life where only Kevin can put you," he'd said. "Because of who he is. And when he does, I won't interfere."

I didn't understand at the time. But now I know. He wasn't talking about stepladders. He was talking about corners, limbs, and all those other places we sometimes find ourselves. Alone. And having to answer to a higher authority than fathers.

That's where I was today. On that stepladder again. I could almost close my eyes and feel the terrible shame of being put up there in disgrace. And I needed Kev. To get me down.

Nastasha stood at the sink preparing formula, her classic good looks frazzled. Her month-old baby, Justin, was in his portable chair on the table, wailing. Was there to be no comfort anywhere in the world today?

"Oh, I'm so glad you're here. I can use you this afternoon."

Nastasha treated me as an equal. I was an adopted

aunt to Justin, had been before he was born when
she'd lived there with my grandmother. She had
taken Nastasha in and given her refuge when she was
pregnant.

I picked Justin up. I was very good with children.
Being the baby in my family, I felt a surge of protect-
iveness in being able to help someone who needed
me for a change.

"I've been up with him all night. He hasn't got his
days and nights straight yet," Nastasha was saying. "I
hope he settles down before the new mothers come."

"Let me feed him."

She gave me the bottle. I sat down holding him.
He smelled so good. "He's just had his bath," she
said. "The water's been turned off all morning,
which didn't help. I think he'll settle down now. If
you take him for a while, I can put the coffee on for
the workmen and finish this platter of sandwiches."

"What's all the stuff on the dining room table?"

She raised her eyes to the ceiling. "You name it.
Canned goods, bread, rice, potatoes. People have
been donating all week. It all has to be put away.
Your brother has a whole underground of sources
when it comes to getting food donated."

"Loaves and fishes, that's what it is!"

Kevin came in the back door, filling the kitchen
with his presence. He went by me, pulling my hair.
"Hey, you look good with a baby in your arms. Don't
let it give you any ideas."

"Hi, Kev."

"Do we have anything cold for the men to drink?" He looked at Nastasha.

He knows, I thought. Somebody's told him already. If he didn't, he'd be looking at me.

"There's soda and beer," she said, "and I'm making coffee. You can take these sandwiches out in a minute."

He took a six-pack out of the fridge, went to a drawer for an opener. "Hullo yourself," he flung over his shoulder. "I thought you were supposed to be camping this weekend." He turned, leaned against the counter, and gave me that lopsided grin of his.

"I guess you heard about it, didn't you, Kev."

"Yeah, I heard. The rectory phone's been ringing since five-thirty this morning. I hope you weren't one of the merrymakers."

I smiled sweetly at him. "Do you think we could talk, Kev?"

"Do we have anything to talk about that can't wait until tomorrow?"

"I think so."

He checked his watch. "I don't know. I'm pretty tied up. I've got two and a half hours before the men quit. They're on time and a half now. Job's gotta be done today. I can't afford double time tomorrow." Again the lopsided grin. "It's important, huh?"

"Yeah, Kev."

"All right, c'mon." He gestured with his head, and

I put the baby back in the portable chair.

"Do you think I should make more sandwiches?" Nastasha asked.

"No." He looked at her. "You're beat. I heard the kid crying. He have you up all night again?"

She nodded.

"Tell him to keep it up until the new mothers arrive. His nighttime serenades will deliver a message better than any I could get across. Why don't you rest? Diana's coming soon. She can help."

"Diana Chaffee?" I couldn't keep the dismay out of my voice.

"Yes, Diana Chaffee." He pulled my hair, still grinning. "Does that present problems to you?"

"She takes up too much of your time. Always mooning over you with those big cow eyes of hers."

"Yeah, well she can moon all she wants. She's been a big help to me in cutting the red tape with social agencies." He picked up the platter of sandwiches and with the six-pack in the other hand, led the way out of the kitchen into the back hall. "C'mon along, well find a corner."

We found a corner out in the hallway. "I don't usually hear confessions with a six-pack in one hand and a platter of sandwiches in the other," he said.

I looked at him entreatingly. He set down the sandwiches and beer on a table in the hallway, came over to where I was leaning against the wall, plunged his hands in his jeans pockets, and leaned with one shoulder against the wall too, looking at me. "Go ahead," he said.

I hesitated. Kev was a good listener. It was part of what he was all about. He knew how to listen and not say anything, just to let somebody talk. He read between the lines when you talked, picked up on things. He was a great jokester, but when you needed him, he was serious. And what I liked best was that lots of times he didn't ask anything of you when he knew you were hurting. He didn't preach or use your temporary weakness to get any points across. I couldn't have stood that. He was so good at what he did. I knew why the line outside his confessional at St. Hedwig's was longer than Father Peterson's, his assistant.

"Kev, I was one of the ones drinking last night."

He nodded.

"I don't know how many beers I had. Maybe four. I got a little sloshed, Kev. The kids were offering them to me, and I didn't want to...to be unsociable. I didn't even like the stuff, that's the thing. And Josh, he's the guy I went with...."

"Josh Falcone?"

"Yeah, do you know him?"

He shook his head, no. "I know his mother. And Gina of course. But he doesn't ever come to church. The mother has mentioned him to me a few times."

"Anyway, Josh got me drinking coffee and washing my face in cold water. So I wasn't that sloshed. But

DiSepio has my name down on a list anyway. A
drunk list at school. Mr. Randolph called Dad this
morning, and Dad freaked and he's acting like I personally put away half a keg. And he says he has to
write an editorial about it. And how can he when his
own daughter is involved?"

"Dad doesn't freak, Brieanna. I've never known
him to do that."

"Well, he's sore."

"That's different. He has reason to be."

"I was all *right* by the time Josh got me home.
That's the thing. Even Dad didn't know I'd been
drinking. He said he's going to school to get my
name off the drunk list. He says I wasn't drunk."

He nodded. "So what's the problem?"

"Well, geez, Kev, it's a bummer. Dad's grounded
me for two weeks, and I don't know what Randolph's
gonna do."

"That still isn't the problem, is it?"

"No."

"What is then?"

"I feel rotten about it, Kev. I really feel awful."

He grinned for the first time. "Good."

"Kev, Dad let me go out with Josh even though he's
eighteen. And Josh is so...decent. He didn't do
anything wrong. He's the one the teachers depended
on. But I'm afraid Dad's gonna blame Josh anyway.
He said he had reservations about letting me go out
with Josh. But that he trusted us."

"Does Dad know Josh was kicked out of military school?"

"You know that?"

"His mother told me. She was really upset about it at the time."

"Did she tell you why?"

"Something about the fact that he got too friendly with the colonel's daughter. Does Dad know that?"

"Uh huh. Josh went and talked to him first. Dad said he was gonna give him another chance."

"Ah. And so now you're hurting because you blew it and ruined Josh's chance. Is that it?"

I nodded. "Kind of, Kev." I looked at him hopefully.

"Yeah, well, I'm sorry this happened, Brie. But I'm glad in a way. I hoped I never had to worry about you and drinking. Other things, maybe, but not drinking. So I never really talked that up to you much. And I know Dad hasn't either. Now, well." He shrugged. "What can I say? You've done it. You've disappointed Dad and yourself. So you see what the consequences of drinking can be."

"You don't have to worry about me drinking, Kev."

"But what led to it?"

"What?"

"You didn't want to be unsociable. That's peer pressure, Brie. That's what I worry about."

"Oh, Kev, you know me better."

"Do I?" And he grinned. "Look, go along with

Dad and be penitent for a while. He'll come around
and let you go out with Josh again. Although I don't
know if I would."

"Why?"

"I'm just kidding." He winked and picked up the
sandwiches and beer. "Look, we'll talk more tomorrow. This is really a bad day. You picked an awful
day. I've gotta run now."

"Sure, Kev." He went out. The door slammed behind him. But for some reason I felt as if I was still
on that ladder. As if he wasn't quite ready to let me
down yet.

"I've put Justin to bed," Nastasha said. "How 'bout
a cup of coffee?"

I sat down at the table and accepted the coffee.
She looked tired, but we chatted a while. She was
excited about the opening of the house and planning
the refreshments for the big day. I listened to her
chat, absentmindedly answering. There had been
something unsatisfactory in the conversation with
Kev. Oh, he'd been nice enough, but this time we
hadn't connected. I felt as if something inside me
was left unraveled.

I supposed it was, because I hadn't told him everything. There were gaps in my appeal for help, and I
think Kev sensed it and, because of the gaps, was unable to deliver for me.

"Oh," Nastasha said, gesturing to the counter,
"have a bun. I forgot they were there. Or do you

want a sandwich? I must be tired. My manners are awful today."

"S'okay, I'll just have a bun," I said, and I got up and went to the kitchen counter.

I wished I hadn't gone to the counter just then. Because over the counter were the windows, their curtains flapping in the September breeze. The windows that looked out on to the backyard.

The backyard where Kevin was. And Diana Chaffee.

If only I hadn't looked just then! I felt a stab of enlightenment (was that what it was?). Looking out at her standing so close to him, in her high heels and trim navy suit, carrying her social worker's briefcase. Their heads were together. Close together. And they were laughing at something. And there was an intimacy in the way they were looking at each other and laughing that made my heart lurch inside me.

Diana and Kevin! Why had I never seen it before? Or had I seen it? Is that what I'd interpreted in her mooning around him? Was I crazy? It couldn't be! How could it be?

Kevin?

We get flashes in life, moments of clarity when we see things as they are. They don't come too often, these flashes of insight. Thank heaven. We wouldn't survive if they did.

Diana and Kevin. Of course! That's why she'd been hanging around so much lately. She was making a play for him! And what about *him?* Didn't he

see it? He didn't look as if he'd been in too much
pain a minute ago there.

I watched them walk across the lawn together.
They look right together, I thought. The way they
walk, they *go with each other.* Why had I been so
blind?

I felt sweat breaking out on my back, I felt a great
roaring in my ears. My heart was thumping like a
rabbit's heart, the way the rabbits had looked at the
4-H fair I'd been to in August. Everything sank inside me. I turned from the counter and took my bun
back to the table and sat down.

Diana and Kevin. My brother, the priest.

"What's wrong?" Nastasha asked.

"I never knew why I hated that woman before.
Now I do."

"She was here all last Saturday," Nastasha said.

I looked at her. Was she too loyal to Kev to say
anything? Or was she just loyal enough to be concerned too?

"Do you see the way she looks at him?" I asked.

Her eyelids lowered. "I see."

"Does he see it?"

"I don't know. Your brother is a very smart man.
Usually nobody puts anything over on him if he can
help it."

"Maybe he can't help it," I said.

"Brie—"

"Nastasha, you *know* how everybody's always saying how handsome he is—how the women always

fool around. My friend Josh says his *mother* wants to run away with Kev! Sure he's joking. But Diana— she's not anybody's mother!"

She sighed. "I know," she said cautiously. "I've been worried, Brie. Don't think I haven't. But I can't believe that your brother..." She hesitated.

"You do believe it, don't you?" I demanded. "You see it too. It isn't just me. Nastasha?"

She shook her head, looked down at her coffee, and didn't answer. I got up. "I bet if I went outside right now, he wouldn't have time for me."

"Brie, he gave you time. Just before."

"He wasn't his usual self. He said he was busy. Now he's outside laughing with Diana."

"Honey, don't push anything. Don't draw any lines and take sides. People have to come down on one side or another when you do, and sometimes they'll come down on the opposite side just to be ornery. Father Kevin is busy right now."

"He sure *is*."

She sighed. "Go," she said, "go outside if you must and rescue your brother."

So I went. I went across the yard to where he and Diana were standing near the Florida room that jutted out from the house.

"Kev?" I approached them hesitantly. They still had their heads together. It took a minute for them to realize I was talking to him. Then they both looked up.

"Hullo," Diana said. "How are you?"

Well, I wasn't going to answer *her!*

"Kev, can I talk to you?"

"Honey, I know I didn't have enough time for you before. But I'm busy."

"But it's important, Kev."

"We did talk before, Brieanna, didn't we?"

"Yes, but there's something else I need to talk to you about. Something I didn't mention before."

He sighed. "Diana has found out about a warehouse in Pennsylvania where there's a lot of food stored. All surplus stuff. They're going to destroy it because the shelf life runs out in a week. If I can get somebody out there, I can have it."

"Kev?" I felt myself trembling inside. Diana was looking at him with such adoration in her eyes. How could she act like that with a priest? And why didn't he see it?

"Are you going there now? To Pennsylvania?"

"If I can't get anybody else to go for me this afternoon, yes, I'll have to go."

"Is Diana going with you?"

"I suppose so, yes. She knows the people who run the place."

"Can I go?"

He looked at me. "I don't know, Brie. You know Dad said you were grounded. Now what do you suppose that means?"

I felt humiliated and childish when he said that. Pennsylvania. Where in Pennsylvania? It was such a

big state. You could drive for hours before you got
where you wanted to go. I bet she'd love that, driving with Kev in his van for hours.

I couldn't allow that, I decided. I had to do something to stop them. I didn't know what, but surely I
could do something. Maybe if I could get him aside
and just talk to him about it, tell him how foolish it all
looked, how even Nastasha had noticed something
between them.

"Kev—"

"You *know* I need the food, Brieanna. For Newark
and for here." He was begging me with his eyes. He
wasn't stupid. He knew what I was up to.

"Now can you understand my urgency?" he asked
softly.

"Can you understand mine?"

He glared at me. Kev can be pushed just so far.
When it comes to a fight, he's up to it. He can get his
Irish up. He uses that righteous anger of his when he
wants to. I've seen him rain it down on kids who
have lied to him or used him. Jesus in the temple,
throwing things. He thinks he has a right to it.

The line Nastasha told me not to draw was drawn
now. And he was coming down on the side of Diana.

"I've got to leave now, Brie," he said quietly.
"We'll take this up tomorrow." He started toward me,
touched my arm. I pulled away and gave him a trem-
ulous look. "You always have time for the kids in
Newark. I've seen you do on-the-spot counseling
with them."

"Do you need on-the-spot counseling?"

"Maybe I do. Maybe you do."

I had his full attention, all right. "I wish I had time. I'd ask you to clarify that last statement." There was an edge in his voice.

"But time is what you don't have, isn't it, Kev?"

"Look, you two," Diana interjected. "If you want to talk to your brother, Brie, for heaven's sake—"

"She doesn't really want to talk to me," Kev said. "That isn't what she's after. Brie, I'm ashamed of you."

"That's nothing compared to what I feel for you."

The workmen in the yard had stopped their chores to overhear this argument between us. If Kev noticed, he didn't say anything. He was putting on his flannel shirt, buttoning it. "I'm sorry, Brieanna. We will talk later. I see we have a great deal to talk about. You need more than on-the-spot counseling."

He took Diana's arm and they started off. The anger I felt was unbelievable. My limbs went weak from it. I watched them go, wanting to run after him and bring him back, beg him not to go, cry, scream, anything. But I didn't. I turned instead and fled across the lawn. I darned near fell into one of the ditches. Before I went into the house, I saw him take her arm and guide her so she wouldn't trip when she got into his van. Then I went into the house, sickened by the whole incident, and threw up.

I threw up until I thought I'd lose something important inside me that was needed to live. Then I leaned over the john, shaking and shivering.

All I could think of was the way Kev had taken her arm and guided her into that van, the protective solicitous way. And the way she'd coyly smiled up at him.

I'd made a fool of myself in front of everybody. I'd acted like a jealous brat because I couldn't tell him what was really bothering me. And what was really bothering me I couldn't accept, couldn't deal with.

Even Nastasha had seen it. I hadn't imagined it. How long had it been going on between them? I felt betrayed.

Kev was a *priest!* So much a priest, so good a priest.

I was only a little girl when he was ordained. But I remember the ceremony in the cathedral. The part that impressed me most was when they wrapped his hands in bands of linen that were annointed with oil. That was the part of the ceremony that made him holy.

The front door bell was ringing. It jolted me back to my senses. I went to answer it. Nastasha must have gone upstairs to nap with the baby. I saw the shadow of a form on the other side of the double frosted glass doors and opened them.

The man who stood there was about twenty-five and dressed in neat slacks, pullover sweater, and tie. His hair was short, and he looked like people in those movies about the fifties. He was dark skinned, probably Spanish. But he spoke English carefully.

"Is Father Kevin in?"

"No." I could still taste the evil stuff in my throat from throwing up. "Can I help you?"

"My name is Manuel. We are friends." He gave me a brilliant smile as if that fact in itself was marvelous. Good for you, I thought. He took an envelope from somewhere inside the sweater and handed it to me.

"I was hoping to see him personally and have a word with him. But it is all right. I know how busy he is."

"Yes, he is," I murmured.

"But I admire him tremendously. He does such good works for people, and we need more like him."

A reply stuck in my throat, got lost in there with the awful taste.

"Do you know if he'll soon be back?"

"He didn't tell me."

"I will try again tomorrow. I know how tied up he is, running the parish. It isn't a job he cares for."

He must be a good friend of Kev's if he knew that, I decided.

He turned to go. "Do you work for him?"

"No, I'm his sister."

Again the face lit up. "Ah, the little sister. He's told me about you."

I smiled and closed the frosted glass door. The phone was ringing now. Well, I certainly wasn't going to stay around all day and be secretary for Kev!

He shouldn't have left the place unattended! I went to answer the phone, thinking that I was doing it as much for Nastasha as for anybody.

"Brie?" It was Josh.

"What?"

"I can't find the stuff."

The stuff. For a moment, my mind couldn't grasp what he was talking about. Yet Josh's voice, so familiar to me by now, brought me back from the uncharted distance I had traveled this morning, brought me up short and to a screeching halt.

"Do you think somebody found it already?" I asked.

"No, but Jim Varney says lots of parents have called to come and get camping gear. Do you remember...?"

"It's the second tree after the path that leads to the river from our campsite."

"It's not there, Brie," he said desolately.

I hesitated, trying wildly to re-create the scene from the night before, but my senses were too fragmented.

"I hate to ask, Brie, but do you think you could come out here and help me find it?"

My head was reeling. And I forgot about Kevin and Diana for a minute. Come out to the island? The sense of urgency was there in Josh's voice. He was *scared,* like he'd been last night when Buetell had thrust the drugs into his hands.

Come out to the island? For just an instant, my

father's face flashed in front of me as it had been at breakfast, forbidding me to go to the island.

But then, overriding all that was the thought of Josh in trouble. And underneath all of it was the dull persistent ache, returning again, the raw, ripped feeling of betrayal that I'd gotten from Kev this morning. And whether it was concern for Josh that motivated me to say yes, I'd come, or anger at Kev, I didn't know. What did it matter, anyway. What did anything matter? If my brother could so callously disregard his vows so that even Nastasha could see it, what was I worried about, disobeying only my father?

I left the envelope from Manuel on Kev's desk and went.

Chapter 8

Was the sun warmer? I didn't notice. Had the day mellowed into something bittersweet that only late September can bring? I didn't notice that, either. All I did notice was that my sweatshirt got too hot after a while so I stopped to take it off, wishing I'd brought some water. I'd thrown up my whole darned lunch. And whether that, in the final analysis, was a result of feeling rotten from too much beer the night before or from fearing the worst about my brother this morning, I didn't know. But I put it down to a combination of both.

Josh was waiting for me at the park entrance. "Hi," he said. He looked as forlorn as I felt.

"Hi."

He took my bike and secured it to a rack.

"You okay?" I asked.

"If I could find the stuff, I'd feel better. How 'bout you? You look beat."

I shrugged. Just what I didn't need was somebody with liquid blue eyes like his asking if I was okay. I was not okay. I was very bad as a matter of fact. But he saw that right off.

"We'll find the stuff," he said. "Don't worry."

"It's not that."

"What is it then?"

I wished his voice didn't brush against the hurting places inside my head so much. I shrugged but could not bring myself to put into words what was wrong. I'd already put it into words with Nastasha. To say it again would give it substance.

"Come on," he urged gently.

"I had a fight with Kev this morning."

"Was it about last night?"

"No. He listened about last night. He was good about that."

"About what then?"

"It's so stinko, Josh."

"Yeah, well this seems to be a day for stinko, so why don't you tell me. No, wait, first we gotta check in with old Jim Varney. He's like a Doberman, you know that? Won't let anybody near the canoe launch until he gives them the okay first."

I stopped in my tracks. "I forgot about Jim Varney. He'll tell my dad we're here."

"Maybe we can sneak you down to the launch since I've already signed in."

"He'll see us," I said dismally.

"We can try, come on."

I told Josh about my morning as we walked to the canoe launch. Jim Varney was nowhere in sight, but I felt as if somebody was watching us just the same.

"Priests do occasionally have flirtations with women, Brie," he said as we got into the canoe. "It goes with the territory." He sounded so mature saying that. Still I protested.

"Not Kev," I said firmly.

"What makes him so different?"

"He is different. You don't know him. He's..." I struggled for words that would describe the dedicated, fun-loving yet spiritual brother I'd known all my life. Tears came into my eyes. "He's just so much a priest. I couldn't imagine him being anything else."

"Then don't. But from what you've told me he's also a very human person. He can't be human in some ways and not in others."

"You're taking his part?"

"No, but it isn't an easy life he's picked, being celibate." He grinned. "I ought to know. Priests are leaving the church all over the place these days because they want to marry. Good ones, too."

"Shut up," I said ungraciously. I didn't want to talk about it anymore. Certainly I didn't want to talk about it with Josh who didn't even know my brother. But I looked at him defiantly as I held on to the sides of the canoe. "What Kev stands for, what he's always been, what he's told me he stands for isn't what he was this morning. That's all I know."

"I'm sorry," Josh said, "but now I'm afraid we have something else to worry about that's worse, Brie. I lied to you about why I wanted you to come here this morning."

I just stared at him, uncomprehending. Worse? What could be worse than what I was feeling about my brother? What was he saying to me now?

"I couldn't tell you on the phone. I had to get you out here, one way or another. I know where you hid the drugs. It's just that somebody else was waiting for me this morning when I got here. Buetell. He found them first. The drugs are worth all kinds of money, Brie."

"How did he know where they were?"

"Oh, hey, it wasn't difficult. He just looked around. He probably watched what direction you ran in last night. Maybe he even followed you, how do we know? The point is he brought them on the camping trip with the intention of burying them and keeping them there. He was gonna ask you if your dad would give permission to let him use the island for fishing. With his dad's boat. Only all this happened. And now he still needs to hide them. And he wants your permission to do it. That's why I called you. He made me."

"He *made* you? How?"

"He said if I didn't he'd take the drugs and tell the police. And with him being on the National Honor

Society and all, nobody would suspect *him*. He's a
student leader. Has a great rep. The rest of the kids
would be in trouble."

"Would he really have done that?"

"I don't know, but I couldn't take the chance. You
think the booze caused trouble, what do you think
would happen if the police knew about drugs?
There's cocaine and everything, Brie."

"And so he wants to get my permission to keep the
stuff here?"

"Yeah." Josh grinned at me sheepishly. "We
walked right into it, Brie. I told you we had trouble.
He's dealing. And he's in heavy with the stuff, and
he's got no place else to keep it. You know how Randolph is coming down on drugs in school."

"Where is he now?"

"On the island. Waiting for us. You don't have to
give in to him, Brie. You don't have to let him keep
his stinking drugs on your island. It's blackmail. I
gave in to him because it isn't my island or my
choice. I couldn't speak for you."

"And if I don't? He could follow through with his
original threat. A lot of innocent kids could get into
trouble."

"So? You're in a mood to be a martyr? You doing
penance or something?"

"Don't be snotty, that isn't it."

"What is it then?"

"I don't know, Josh. I'm pretty confused," I admitted. "I don't even know why I came here this morn-

ing. I almost didn't. My dad would kill me if he knew I was here, and he could *still* find out about it."

"You came because I asked you to come."

"I'm not so sure about that. I came because I was disgusted with Kev and what would ordinarily bother me didn't bother me because of that. But I'm here now, and I only know I can't let all those kids get in trouble on account of me."

He rowed in silence for a while. "You sure about that? You know what you're getting into, letting him keep the stuff here? Maybe he's just giving us idle threats. Maybe we should call his bluff. Whoever he's working for could make things pretty rough for him if he turns the stuff in. We gotta think about that."

"I don't know, Josh. He must be desperate. Desperate people do awful things. We have to think about that too."

The canoe was nearing the dock. Josh guided it in and jumped out and secured it. "You're pretty mature for your age," he said.

"I don't feel very mature this morning." I jumped out and stood on the dock looking around the familiar landscape of my island, quiet and peaceful in the September sun. "Where is he?"

"Oh, he's here watching us. You can be sure of that."

A chill went through me in spite of the sun's warmth. "Look," Josh said, "maybe we can make some demands too. Sort of negotiate, if you're intent on doing this. Personally, I think you should tell him to take a flying leap, but if you wanna go along with him to keep the lid on things, I think you oughta push to give him a time limit. Have him get the drugs off the island by a certain date."

"Do you think I could do that?"

"It's *your* island!" Josh's voice cracked with indignation. "Of course you can. Make him sweat a little bit. Don't forget, you can blow the whistle on him anytime. He knows that. Come on, I'll help you out. I'll back you up."

Buetell wasn't anything the way I thought he would be about it. I don't know how I thought he would be, menacing, probably. After all, the whole idea of him dealing in drugs was menacing enough.

"Hello, McQuade."

Looking at him, poised on a rock above the dock, I was almost surprised to notice he hadn't developed two heads overnight. He looked the same as he had yesterday, as innocuous, as clean, as untainted and ordinary. He didn't even need a shave. His eyes weren't bleary, and I found the story that he was dealing in drugs hard to believe.

"Hullo," I said.

"He tell you what I want?" He motioned to Josh.

"Yeah. He told me." I stood on the dock, my hands in the back pockets of my jeans. Buetell just kept

right on with what he was doing while he spoke to
me. And what he was doing was pitching stones. He
had a bunch of them piled up next to him, and he
would send them skimming out across the river. He
was very good at it. Like Tom Sawyer or somebody.

"Look, I don't know what else to do," he said. "I'm
stuck with more stuff than I bargained for."

He sounded like a newsboy with too many papers
to deliver. "That must be a pretty heavy bargain," I
said.

"Yeah." Another stone got pitched. "Well, that's
another story. Thing is that this batch is it. That's
what I told them anyway."

"Told who?"

"Never mind who." One stone must have done a
particularly exceptional job of skipping over the
water because he gave a yell. "Hey, did you see
that?" We looked in silent admiration while he se-
lected another and gave a repeat performance, as the
stone skimmed the water in skips and jumps.

"Thing is I'm gonna sell this batch of stuff off," he
said. "Then I'm outa the business. I want to ask you
if I could keep it here for a while. Get your old man
to okay my using your island. Maybe you could tell
him I'm using my dad's boat for fishing. I was gonna
bury the stuff here last night, only I almost got caught
with it. Then after you took it off everybody's hands
so bravely last night, I came out here in my dad's boat
this morning and found it. I would have buried it all

over again and asked you if I could use the island for fishing. You never would have known the difference, only soldier boy got here this morning right after I did."

"What makes you think I would let you use my island for fishing, anyway?" I said sullenly.

He grinned. "Hey, McQuade, anybody who did what you did last night, anybody as quick thinking as *that,* is pretty with it. You're no nerd. That's how I figured it."

I felt the color suffuse my face at his praise. I had been good last night, even I gave myself credit for that. But why did I feel so good when some lowlife like Barry Buetell said so? I was starting to worry about myself. There was something about me, I decided, that wanted the approval of the Barry Buetells of this world. I wanted to be considered cool and with it. Even more than I wanted the approval of my dad and Kevin.

"Soldier boy here," he went on, pitching another stone into the water, "wanted to ditch the stuff in the river. I hadda tell him the trouble I'd be in if he did."

"Trouble?"

He grinned. "Yeah. The kind of trouble that a nice little girl like you wouldn't know anything about. Like, you might come out here some day and come across me buried on your island. You wouldn't want anything like that to happen to me, would you, McQuade?"

"No. I guess not. Not even to you, Buetell."

"Well, that's why I hadda get you out here this morning."

I hesitated, looking at Josh, who was just sitting there on the ground listening to this exchange without saying anything. "Would you really have told the police there were drugs here if I didn't come when Josh asked?"

His smile faded. "Look, McQuade, if you don't let me keep the drugs here, the police are still gonna know. I'll call them and tell them I came out here this morning to get my camping gear and found drugs. My background is spotless. My dad's a member of the town council, a local businessman, and he buys tickets for the policeman's ball every year. Belongs to the Elks too. They'll never suspect me."

"I think you stink," I said.

"Yeah, well I like you too, honey. But that's just the way things are."

I fell silent for a moment. Buetell kept right on pitching those stones. I looked at Josh. He got up slowly and squinted over at Buetell.

"If she does it," Josh said, "if she agrees, you have to agree to some stuff too."

Buetell laughed. "You her manager or something?"

"I'm her friend," Josh said. His gaze was steadfast and his voice unwavering enough so that when his eyes met Buetell's, Barry pulled his eyes away first.

"What do you want, Falcone?"

"You have to agree to sell the stuff off fast. Get rid of it as fast as you can," Josh said firmly. "You also have to agree not to have people tracking onto the island. That would make the state suspicious. And..."

He took a deep breath and continued. "You have to promise that if you get caught Brie is out of it."

I held my breath. Buetell said nothing for a moment. He just pitched another stone, fiercely this time. "Why should I agree to all this?"

"Because you want something from Brie," Josh said. "And there has to be something given in return. She's putting herself on the line for you. You're desperate."

Another stone skimmed the water. "Yeah, well, how do I know she won't go to her old man the newspaper editor? Or her brother, the priest. And blow the whistle on me."

"You'll have to trust each other," Josh said. "It seems to me that's what you'll have to do."

"Can I trust you, McQuade?" Buetell said to me.

"You can trust me. What about you?"

"Hell." And he tossed another stone. "I'm taking more of a chance than you are. Okay. I'll have the stuff sold off in a month. And nobody but me comes here to get it. And if I get caught, I get caught. You're out of it."

"All right," I said.

He got up and wiped his hands on the seat of his jeans. "You gotta keep your part of the bargain too," he said.

"I have no reason not to, Buetell."

He nodded. "You're okay. You know that? I never would have believed it of you."

"Yeah. I'm terrific. I never would have believed it of me either," I answered. And once again I felt a glow of satisfaction at his approval.

I had more troubles when we left the island. As we disembarked in the state park, some parents were coming to retrieve the camping gear. Debbie Geyer's mother and father recognized me right off. He worked in Dad's composing room, so I knew he would drop the news on my father, maybe before Monday. I felt a sense of dread. But what else could I have done? If I hadn't gone to the island, not only Debbie Geyer, but all the other kids would have been in eight different kinds of trouble.

As Kev had told me so often, you don't get any thanks for doing a good thing in the world. You have to just settle for the warm feeling that accompanies the acts. But I didn't even have that as I watched Josh tie my bike onto the roof of his car.

Chapter 9

Josh dropped me within two blocks of my house and loosened my bike from the top of his car. Slowly I pedaled home. It was almost five o'clock, and I didn't realize how hungry I was until I caught the smell of Alma's cooking. I left my bike in the backyard, careful to keep it out of the entranceway because that would set my father off faster than anything. Then I went in. Alma's back was to me. She was at the table fixing salad. I went over to the stove to sample whatever was in the pot.

"Outa there," she said without turning around. "Your daddy's been looking for you. Where you been?"

"Hanging out."

"Well, you better get yourself in there and see him. He's been wondering where you've been doing this hanging out of yours. You been with that boy again?"

"Oh, Alma!"

She turned around, regarding me with that serene black face of hers that never changed. I can't remember Alma ever looking any different, any younger or any older, since I was a baby. She had been with my mom and dad since before then. And although she loved my mom something fierce, it was my dad she stayed with when Mom left. Because of us kids, she'd said. But I know it was because she couldn't bear to leave my dad with three children. She may have loved my mom, but my dad she respected.

"You'd better not use that tone on your father. He got a phone call about half an hour ago, and he told me that the minute you come through that door, you're to go in to him. Now go on, get."

"Is he mad, Alma?"

She turned her back and went back to peeling vegetables. "It seems to me that you had him mad enough last night. It would seem to me that you'd know when to quit making him mad. That's what it seems to me."

I longed to throw my arms around her, to lose myself in the comfortable folds of her ample body as I'd done so much as a child. Where had I been? Drugs, Alma, out helping somebody conceal drugs. I wished I was five years old again. I wished she could still take me upstairs and wash the dirt off me and put me in my pajamas and tuck me in. That's what I wished. But I said nothing. I just went past her in the kitchen, smelling her familiar talcum. It affected me the same as the fragrance of Kev's cassock affected me. It made me dizzy with wanting to be small and secure again.

My dad was in his study at the end of the hall. He was reading in his favorite leather chair. He glanced up when I stood in the doorway.

"Where have you been, Brie?" The tone was super casual.

"Hi, Daddy."

He closed the book and set it aside. He knocked the ashes from his pipe in a nearby ashtray. "You were supposed to be home before this."

"I didn't know there was a set time I was supposed to be home."

"I don't remember giving you permission to galli-vant all day."

"I wasn't gallivanting, Daddy."

"You've been with that boy? That's where you've been?"

"I just went for a ride on my bike."

"Are you lying to your old dad, Brie? Is that what you're doing?"

The question was light, easy, but the voice was de-ceiving. The question was loaded. There was no parent in the world more decent or fair than my fa-ther. Because he was like that, he hated indecency and unfairness and lies. In his paper, he devoted his life to fighting lies. I'd often seen him at his best doing so and was glad his vehemence wasn't directed

at me. Because I knew there was a very real core of
anger behind his outward gentleness. I'd experienced it a few times, enough to let me know I didn't
want to tap into it.

"You might as well come in here and tell me." He
started to fill his pipe. I went into the paneled room
where he spent so much of his time. It had deep
green area rugs over honey-colored wood floors, lots
of books and leather and brass. The walls were covered with his newspaper awards. He gestured that I
should sit on the ottoman next to him.

"I guess you already know, don't you, Daddy."

"Yeah, I know." He considered the pipe. "I told
you I didn't want you seeing him again, didn't I?"

"Daddy, I had a good reason."

"Well, why don't you tell it to me. See how good it
is."

"I left my wallet on the island last night. Josh took
me over in the canoe to get it. You wouldn't have
wanted me going across alone, would you?"

"Where is the wallet?"

"It's...out in my backpack in the basket of my
bike," I lied.

He looked at me steadfastly. My father can play as
good a game as anybody when the occasion warrants
it. "Why don't you go get it?" he said.

I stood rooted in the middle of the room. It was as
if we were locked in some crazy game, the two of us,
each of us not wanting to play but refusing to give
up. I knew one thing, my father would never give

up. Nobody got the best of him. To try was sheer insanity. And I knew something else too. The more I kept at it the angrier he'd get.

"I can't get it," I said dismally.

"Why not?"

"'Cause it's not in the backpack. It's upstairs."

He nodded, satisfied, the pipe clenched in his teeth like General MacArthur. The fragrance of it filled the room. I had always loved the smell of his tobacco. He raised his eyes to look at me. He looked so sad. "You know I hate lying, Brie."

"I know."

"I give you a lot of leeway around here. I don't expect you to sneak behind my back and lie. Now why did you go there today?"

"I can't tell you."

"Can't? Or won't?"

"I don't wanna lie anymore. So I can't."

"Try the truth then."

I shook my head, no. Then I turned and started for the door.

"Don't leave this room, Brie." He didn't raise his voice. He didn't have to. He did get up though. The door of his study was half open, and I was holding the knob. He leaned against the door, closing it. "Did you have a fight with your brother today?"

I was starting to tremble. This was too much for me. He was going to start on my fight with Kev now too. "Yes."

"About what? Can you tell me that?"

"About nothing. We just fought."

He nodded. "What am I supposed to think you were doing on that island with Josh Falcone?"

Somehow, through some miraculous drawing of strength from resources I didn't know I had, I managed to look up at him.

"I don't know. What is there to think?"

"I can tell you what Jim Varney was thinking. What he suggested to me."

So Varney had seen me. "What?" I gulped.

"He's a good man, Varney, but he likes to gossip. It's probably all over town right now. He says lots of parents went out to the island this morning to get camping gear. He says you and Falcone were the only kids. He says you had no camping gear when you came back to the state park."

"I don't care what he says."

"Well I do. I care what people say about my daughter."

"People are always going to *say* things, Daddy. Are you gonna believe them? Or me?"

"You haven't told me anything I can even hope to believe yet, Brieanna. And unfortunately, with the reputation Falcone has..." He shrugged and walked back to his chair and sat down.

"Daddy..."

He raised those brown eyes of his. "Yes?"

"I...can't tell you now why I went there today. You just have to trust me, please."

"I'm sorry, Brie." The tone was sad, apologetic. "I can't accept anything less from you now but the truth. I *did* trust you. Unless you can come up with some reasonable explanation, I'm in a pretty bad position. I can't defend you if somebody passes a snide remark. How am I supposed to feel?"

"How do you feel?" I asked.

"I don't know." He shifted his weight in the chair and studied me. "I thought I knew you, Brie, before you came home and admitted you were drinking. I chalked it up to a mistake. Then you ran off against my wishes with that boy again—after I expressly forbade you to go to the island. I'm thinking that maybe I don't know you at all anymore. So I don't know how I feel or what I believe at the moment."

Tears came to my eyes. I turned to go.

"I said don't go out that door, Brie. If you think I'm fooling around, try me." The tone was still soft, but it was as cold as ice. And inside me, I felt the same cold and an awful sense of loss.

"No more now," he said gently. "This has gone far enough. I'm not getting anywhere with you, and you're not yourself right now. You're tired and hungry. I'm not going to discuss this with you any further. Trouble with me is I allow you to have your say too much. There's been too much discussion around here. I'm still the parent, and I'm simply going to punish you as you deserve."

I stood silent, waiting. I knew how difficult it was

for my father to act the stern parent. But when his anger got the best of him, he could manage it very nicely.

"You're confined to the house. School and home. That's it. That includes seeing Kev. You gotta ask me first. About anything."

I couldn't believe it. "For how long?"

"Until you come to me, voluntarily, and tell me what you were doing on the island today. Now go wash up for supper."

I just stared at him. The undue harshness of what he had just said made me want to cry. "Daddy—"

"You don't *get* it, Brie. There is no bargaining. You've given up your right to do that. You want to go to the library or *anywhere*, you ask permission. Now I want to eat. I'm hungry. Go wash up."

"I don't want any supper."

He got up and came toward me. "No hysterics or hunger strikes," he said calmly. "I can sell that island. You could have a nice little tidy sum in your trust fund from it. The state's been after me to sell it. They want to make it a part of the park. You want me to do that? Is that what I have to do to make you mind?"

I looked at him, still dumbstruck. "No."

"Then behave. You've given me enough trouble. I never had half the trouble raising your brother or sister as I've had with you."

I felt the resentment rising in my throat. "Ceil left

you," I flung at him. "She didn't want to live with you anymore."

I know how that hurt him. He turned his face partially away and set down his pipe, but he didn't betray the hurt he felt.

"Yeah," he said. "Well Ceil was here until she was seventeen, and she never gave me any trouble. And neither did Kev."

"You didn't think Kev was so wonderful when he became a priest," I said.

He whirled on me. "We're not discussing Kev now. We're discussing you! And you fall short of everything for me today! And don't talk about your brother like that! You ought to have some respect for his priesthood. The trouble is he lets you get away with too much. Well, that's between you and him. But when you're around me, I won't have you demeaning what he is. You hear?"

I withered under his look. "I was only saying, Daddy, that he disappointed you when he became a priest. I was only remembering that."

"Yes, he did." His voice got gentler. He plunged his hands into his trouser pockets, and his face got very sad. "But he's so good at it. And I realize now that he couldn't be anything else, that he made the right decision. He's a rare being, Kevin is, a good human being and a good priest. You don't often meet that combination. I've suffered a loss in not being able to have him in the newspaper business, but because of that, what he is means twice as much to me. And I won't hear your putting him down. Even in jest. Remember that."

I knew by the look on his face what Kevin's priesthood meant to him. And I thought, with a fresh stab of fear and remorse, of Kevin and Diana. "Yes, Daddy," I said.

We had a quiet supper, he and I. We had little to say to each other, although he was polite. All the while, my head was spinning with everything that had happened in the last twenty-four hours. I knew one thing. I had to do something so Buetell could get to the island.

After supper, I knocked on the door of Dad's room. He was dressing for a date with Amanda. He opened the door and walked back inside to adjust his tie in front of the mirror. "What is it, Brie?"

He was a very handsome man. It was a fine pin-striped suit he was wearing. And even though he was fifty-three, he was definitely what Gina would call distinguished.

"Can I talk to you?"

"You can talk to me any time you want, you know that."

"I know you don't want to hear anything else about the island today, but Barry Buetell from school wants to use it once in a while for fishing. He uses his dad's boat for fishing a lot."

He was still fussing with the tie. "Go on."

"I said he could. I mean, I said I'd ask you if he could."

He scooped his change off the dresser and put it in his pants pocket. He reached for his suit jacket. The lamp light shone on the silver in his hair. He switched off the light and came into the hall. "Buetell. The name sounds familiar."

"His father owns the sports store in town. He's on the National Honor Society."

"Oh yeah. Good man. Sponsored the Little League with uniforms, the father. Now there's the kind of boy you ought to be going out with, Brie. On the National Honor Society. How come you don't bring boys like that around here?"

I couldn't believe it. "He's a jerk."

"Well, I'm sure jerks don't make the National Honor Society. Sure, he can use the island once in a while. No parties, though."

"No, Daddy. No parties. If Jim Varney calls, will you tell him it's okay?"

"Yes, Brie, I'll be sure to do that."

Chapter 10

On Monday morning, Mr. Randolph got on the horn at school to make his usual boring announcements. What saved them from being boring on Monday morning, however, was his rendition of the trouble on the senior trip.

"Some students cannot enjoy privileges without abusing them," he said. He wasn't much good at face-to-face dialogue, but somehow when he got on the loud speaker at school he took on another personality, using just the right dramatic pauses between his sentences. Usually, we had a lot of fun listening to him, but this morning everybody was pretty grim.

"I will personally meet with those students on Mr. DiSepio's list after school today in my office," he said.

I hadn't talked to Gina since our argument. In the lunchroom, I saw her with Debbie Geyer and Hope

Giangrasso. Usually, Gina and I ate lunch together. I was with some kids from my art class. Everybody in the lunchroom was talking about the kids on Di-Sepio's list. Being on that list had become a status symbol, nothing less. A dubious one to me. I was miserable. I felt a total blackness creeping over me, not only about being on the list but about what I had done.

It had been with me since I woke up, that blackness. The realization of the deal I'd struck with Buetell sickened me. Had I been crazy? All morning as I dressed, ate, got myself to school, I tried to integrate it into my life.

It wouldn't integrate. I never should have let Buetell talk me into it! At the time, it seemed so right. Still, what else could I have done? Let Buetell call the police? Get everybody into trouble? The moment those thoughts crossed my mind I dismissed them. I was too much a Catholic, too much a priest's sister not to realize I was making excuses.

The end never justifies the means. Kev had taught me that since I was old enough to understand the meaning of the words. That was one of Kev's commandments, a very basic one, and I'd gone against it outright.

The bell for classes rang and the other kids from my table scrambled off. I watched Gina get up and walk her tray to the conveyor belt, then wander over to my table.

"So. You're on DiSepio's list?"

I said nothing. I couldn't believe she was even talking to me.

"I told you if you went out with my brother you'd get into trouble."

My eyes widened. "Gi, Josh had nothing to do with my drinking. He didn't even know I was doing it. He was as upset as my dad when he found out!"

She ignored that. "If you have an ounce of brains in your head, you'll stay away from him, Brie. I don't know how else to tell you."

"Thanks for the warning. You already did that. I find your brother to be a very nice, decent person. And I don't want to hear anymore about him."

She made as if to move away, but then she hesitated. "What did your dad say?"

She liked my dad. She used to hang around the house all the time.

"I'm grounded."

"That's *all?*"

"It's practically house arrest. I can't go anywhere without asking."

"What'd Kev say?"

"I don't wanna talk about Kev." She loved Kev. She was crazy about him, and he always treated her just like he treated me. He was good with young people.

"I'll bet he just loved it, your drinking," she said sarcastically.

"Yeah, he got a kick out of it. He rolled on the floor laughing."

"You really let everybody down, didn't you?"

"Shove it, Gi."

"I don't feel a bit sorry for you. You like Josh, don't you?"

The question brought me up short. "Yes, I do."

"I wish you wouldn't."

"I know that. You've made it perfectly clear."

"For you, I mean, I wish you wouldn't. I know you hate me right now. I've acted pretty awful to you."

"I don't hate you, Gina. But you have acted awful. It's not like you. I know you're possessive of your brother, but after all, he's not—"

"He's not what?"

I reached wildly for words. "He's not a *priest!* You can't keep him in hiding. I can't even tell Kev what to do, and *he's* a priest!"

"I have my reasons," she said. "I don't care. You'll find them out someday. I wish you wouldn't, but you will."

She turned to go. I watched her walk off, feeling more alone than ever, trailing behind her all the tender memories of our growing up together. I picked up my tray. I'd be late for science if I didn't hurry, and then I'd be in more trouble.

"This little scandal of ours was in both area newspapers this morning," Mr. Randolph said. He barely moved his mouth when he spoke, and I was reminded of the Wizard in the Wizard of Oz with his wind machine. Mr. Randolph wasn't very impres-

sive without his microphone. It was his wind machine. With his black-rimmed glasses and bald head,
he looked like a wax dummy in a museum.

"One newspaper made it the subject of its editorial." His eyes slid over to me as he said this. "And,
while that says a lot for fair journalism, since Mr.
McQuade's daughter was involved, it does little for
our school. Our school's name has been sullied. Because of this I am imposing in-school suspension for
all of you for two weeks. There will be no participa-
tion in extra-curricular activities for that time. And
you will not attend classes. You will do your work in
a detention room, and if you lose credits, then you
lose credits. You will have to make them up later.
That will be all."

We shuffled out. Josh was waiting in the outer office, because he was doing a story on this for the
Close Call.

"I guess my dad's editorial didn't help any," I said.

"Your dad did what he had to do, Brie. Like you
did with Buetell."

"I'd rather not talk about what I did with Buetell
right now if it's all the same to you."

"Randolph is setting the tone for the school year.
He's got to make an example of you kids. Listen,
Brie, I feel just as responsible as you for this thing
with Buetell. And I,m gonna keep on him to move
the stuff. As quick as he can. I'm as guilty as you are
about it."

"It's my island," I reminded him.

"But I was there with you. I'm an accomplice. I'm in this with you, Brie." He took my hand, something he rarely did. "Come on, don't look so grim, we're in this together."

"I asked my dad if Buetell could use the island for fishing. He said yes. He said that's the kind of boy I should be dating. He liked the idea of the National Honor Society."

"Holy—"

"Yeah, I know."

He sighed. "We won't be able to see each other much with your in-school suspension."

"I know. And we won't be able to see each other out of school. I told you what my dad did to me."

"We'll think of something," he promised. "Hey, guess what. We put Confucius out in the flight cage. He's flying, exercising his flight muscles. He's doing great. We ought to be able to let him free by Halloween."

"Oh, I want to see him again! I want to see the other animals, too, Josh. But my dad won't let me go anywhere if I don't tell him why I was on the island. And I can't tell him anything at all."

"We'll think of something," he said again.

"Maybe we can." I brightened. "Maybe we could think up a good lie, Josh."

"Another lie? That's all he needs. Better you don't say anything."

"But—"

"Ssh. Listen, just cool it for a while. Let's let Buetell get the stuff off the island first. Let's give it awhile. Then we'll think of something to tell your dad, I promise."

Things could get no worse. By the end of the first week of in-school suspension, I was lonely and depressed. I saw nobody but Mr. DiSepio who conducted the class each day as if we were in maximum-security prison. We were allowed out only to go to the bathroom. We had to bring lunch from home and eat at our desks. Milk or soda was delivered to the class. We had to go to our homeroom first each morning to get assignments the teachers had left and return the work to our homerooms after school. We had no contact with our other teachers, and if we didn't understand the assignments, that was tough luck. We were on our own. Like Mr. Randolph had said, if we lost credit, we'd have to make it up.

By Friday, I was almost out of my tree.

I missed Josh so much I felt like I had a toothache inside me. But he called every night, and I managed to see him for a couple of minutes after school. By Friday, I had invented six new lies I was ready to tell my father about why Josh and I had been on that island. But Josh wouldn't let me. "Since I'm implicated, you'll have to clear any lies with me," he teased, "and I'm not about to approve any right now."

By Friday night, I was in a stupor of resentment and bitterness over the whole thing, not to mention worry about Buetell. He'd been evading Josh all week, and I had no chance of catching up with him.

"It isn't fair," I told my father Friday night at supper.

"What isn't fair?"

"In-school suspension."

"You earned it."

My father's sense of fairness did not coincide with mine. My sense of fairness was concerned with my hair being straight while Kev's curled up in back and my eyes being brown while his were blue. And my breasts being nowhere as prominent as those of most of the girls in the junior class. It had to do with the fact that every other girl in school had a mother to register her older sister's silver pattern at Hornby's downtown when she got engaged.

My father's sense of fairness had to do with toxic-waste dumps and teachers getting tenure when they didn't deserve it. And leash laws. He was absolutely gung ho over leash laws.

I decided to try another approach. "Daddy, do you think Josh could come over for an hour tonight? He's awfully good at geometry, and he was helping me with mine before all this happened. And I need help."

"Your brother Kevin is good at geometry too."

"But Kev's so busy."

"No, Brie. He can't."

"I don't suppose you care that I'm going crazy."

"You can have your privileges back tomorrow if you'll just tell me what you were doing on that island. This has become a contest of wills between us, Brie. I didn't want that. But since it has, I'm determined you're not going to get the best of me. I've talked this over with your brother, and he agrees it's the only thing I can do."

Kev! A light went on inside me. A small one but a light nevertheless. Kev would be able to help me! Why hadn't I thought of Kev? Daddy listened to Kev. If I could get the smiling Irish priest to soften him up...

"Daddy, could I go see Kevin tomorrow?"

"You fought with him as I recall. I told you a couple of times that he asked for you. You didn't seem to care. You never even went to the opening of Second Chance. He felt bad about that. He thinks you're avoiding him."

"I couldn't get out of school, Daddy. Mr. Randolph said the only way he'd let us out of in-school suspension was with a doctor's note or because of a death in the family."

"I would have called him and gotten you off. I do have some clout at that school, you know."

"I didn't want to be a special case, Daddy. It wouldn't have been fair to the other kids."

He eyed me as if he knew I was lying. The fact was I hadn't wanted to go to Kev's old grand opening.

"I just thought, Daddy, that Kev could give me some help with the geometry. You wouldn't want me to fail, would you?"

"All right," he agreed. "You can go there tomorrow. But he's under a lot of pressure. This parish work isn't his cup of tea. I'm worried that he's working too hard. So don't be a nuisance and don't start any trouble."

Chapter 11

The office of Second Chance was in the Florida room. My grandmother used to receive people there, because she was known to everyone and very active in community service. Kev used it just as she'd left it. He kept her white Queen Anne desk and her plants and white wicker furniture. All he'd added were the white file cabinets and a typewriter. When he was working in Newark, he'd come for the weekend and spend Saturday afternoons there. Now I think he used it to escape from the constant demands of parish life.

"Kev-IN." The woman's voice stopped me dead in the hall. It was her. Diana. Why wasn't she calling him Father Kevin?

"C'mon," he was saying. "I'll take the coffee. I was only teasing. You make great coffee."

I paused outside the door. She was perched on the

end of the desk in a pose Gina would call provoca-
tive. He was leaning back in his chair wearing the
black cassock he wore when he heard confessions. It
was very dramatic looking and made him look taller.
I happened to know that he wore it over his jeans and
T-shirt, with sneaks on his feet.

"The coffee is good," he said. "What is it?"

"It's decaffeinated in water. Almond mocha. I paid
ten dollars a pound for it."

"You'll have to let me reimburse you."

"Don't be silly. You've done so many favors for
me."

I felt my skin crawl. I can tell a lot by the tone of
people's voices. Kev was using what I called his velvet tone now, like when you talked to him about
something that was special and he was being sympa-
thetic. I must have made a sound in the doorway,
because they both looked up, saw me, and smiled.
Diana slipped off the desk.

"Well, if it isn't the delinquent?" Kev said. "Who
let you out?"

Diana grabbed her things. "I'd better go."

"You don't have to." He got up. "We still have that
grant application to go over."

"There's time yet. I'll call you next week. Hello,
Brieanna."

I didn't answer her. She smiled at Kev. "I think
your little sister has something on her mind." The
way she said it made me want to trip her.

He stood watching her leave, then turned to

straighten some papers on his desk. "C'mon in."

I went in and sat down in a wicker chair.

"How are you, Brieanna?"

"I'm okay."

"I wish you'd be a little polite to Diana."

"I wasn't fresh. I didn't say anything."

He smiled at me knowingly. "You can be just as hurt by another person not saying anything as by that person being fresh."

I said nothing.

"Well." He grinned. "Anyway I'm glad to see you. We missed you at the opening. You had a lot to do with this house. I kind of wanted you to be here."

"I couldn't get out of school."

"Did you try?"

That's something Dad hadn't thought of asking. "No."

He nodded, satisfied with the truth. "You want some coffee?" He gestured to the coffee maker. "Darned stuff is ten dollars a pound. But I'm getting off caffeine. I've been too uptight. Been getting heart palpitations. You believe it? I'm thirty-one, and I've got a jumpy heart."

"Did you go to the doctor?"

"Yeah. He told me to get off the coffee. I was up to about eight cups a day. Told me to get off the cigarettes too, but..." He shrugged and smiled impishly. "I have no other vices. He said it's nothing to worry about. How are you, anyway? I hear old man Randolph really came down on you kids."

"Yeah, he's making an example of us." I got up and helped myself to the coffee, seeing an opening. "But it's what Dad's doing that's driving me nuts. He's got me under house arrest. I had to get permission to come here today! I can't do anything. It's ridiculous."

He lit a cigarette and sat down. The match illuminated his face, and I could see, around his eyes, how tired he was. He flicked the match out. "You know what he wants from you, don't you?"

"I can't. I can't tell him, Kev."

"You can't? Or you won't?"

"What?"

"Dad seems to think this has become a contest of wills between you. If it has, you won't win with him. He's a tough nut, Dad is. He doesn't give, he doesn't crack."

"Geez, Kev, do you think I'd do this to myself just to get the best of Dad? I can't tell him right now, that's all."

He looked at me cautiously, from beneath those fringed black lashes of his, those Irish lashes that the women found so appealing. "People have been saying things to him about you and that boy. Intimating things. That's getting to him. He's proud of his kids. It hurts."

"Yeah, well people oughta mind their own business. And don't call him that boy. He's got a name."

He spread his hands in a conciliatory way. "All right, all right. Calm down. Dad just doesn't like hearing those things about his daughter. It's come to him from a few sources already."

"Well, he's a newspaperman. He should know better than to accept hearsay."

He smiled wryly. "I guess it's hard for parents sometimes."

"And what about you?"

"Me?" He focused those innocent blue eyes on me. Tired as they were, I could see something in them, some question, badly concealed. "I'm here. Just the way I always am. I'm one great big ear, Brieanna."

"Well, you weren't last week."

"Last week?"

"You don't remember last week? When we fought? I wanted to talk to you. Out in the yard with Diana."

"Oh, yeah, I'm sorry about that, Brie. I had lots on my mind."

I leaned forward in the chair. The casual tone irritated me. "You're *sorry*? You're a priest! When people need you, you can't just walk away and say, a week later, that you're sorry."

"Hey, wait a minute, I didn't know you needed me as a priest that day. I thought I was just being your brother. What are you laying on me?"

I glared at him. How can you love somebody so much and have that love turn to hatred so quickly? It frightened me. I know they say hate is the flip side of love, so it scared me to see how quickly I became angry with Kev. "I didn't care about anything after we fought," I said. "I felt sick over it. I went into the house and threw up."

"You threw up because you were feeling sick from your beer drinking the night before. That's why you threw up."

I ignored that. "I really felt betrayed, Kev. Over what happened."

"Nothing happened. Except in your mind."

"Josh called me right after that and asked me to go to the island. I went. I know I shouldn't have, but I didn't care."

He looked at me very deliberately for a full moment. Studied is more the word for it. Then he flicked some ashes from his cigarette. "So you're gonna blame me for whatever happened that day, is that it?"

"I'm not blaming you."

"I'd like to know what else you just did. Look, I'm an old hand at this. I hear it in confession all the time. I've been unfaithful to my wife because she doesn't understand me. I robbed the liquor store because my old man beat me when I was a kid. C'mon, Brie, you know I don't buy that garbage. This is Kevin you're talking to. Old Kev, the guy you used to tell everything to. The same wonderful guy who listened to all your troubles and insecurities, who helped you work through the rough spots about Mom. Who gets you out of all your scrapes with Dad. You can tell me anything you want, and I won't be judgmental or shocked. I've heard it all in confession. Only don't give me any garbage, Brie. Because I know the difference. And I deserve better."

It got very quiet in the room with only the clock ticking. I sipped my coffee. It had gotten cold. He took a final drag on his cigarette and mashed it out in an ashtray.

"Now what do you want?" he said softly.

"What?"

"Why did you come here today? You didn't come to the opening. You stayed away. But you're here now. You want me to run interference for you with Dad? That it?"

I couldn't fool him. Whatever they did to him at the seminary they did well, because he knew about people. He knew how to read them, how to handle them. I nodded mutely.

He got up to get more coffee. I studied his back, hoping to find some reassurance in the dramatic lines of the cassock that flowed from shoulder to floor. He stirred in sugar, then sat down. "What do I have to work with?"

"What?"

"What do I go in to him with if I plead your case? You haven't told me anything yet either."

"Well, geez, Kev, you know I wouldn't have sex with anybody."

"I don't know anything, Brieanna. Except what you tell me."

"Well, I didn't."

"Okay. Now I know what you didn't do. You wanna tell me what you did do that day?"

"I can't."

He let his breath out in a sigh. "We're back to square one then."

"I can't tell any adult."

The blue eyes widened, the only indication of surprise. The face stayed the same.

"There's only one way I could tell you. In the confessional."

Now pinpricks of disbelief appeared in the blue eyes. But still he said nothing. He let me continue.

"That's the only way, Kev. So you couldn't tell anybody."

"Don't you trust me, Brieanna?"

I found it difficult to see what was in the blue eyes now. So I didn't look at them. I looked away. "It isn't that. You'd *have* to tell. You're an adult."

I had to admire his cool. The voice got smoother. "That's what you want, Brieanna? Confession? Is that why you're here?"

I shook my head, no.

"You want confession, it's all right with me. I never asked you, because I never thought you wanted..."

"No." I got up quickly to get more coffee. "I didn't say that's what I wanted. I said that's the only way I could tell you." I busied myself with the coffee. I couldn't stand the look in his eyes, the look of decency and intelligence and confusion.

"I hate to think of you carrying around something so heavy inside you."

"It's okay. It'll work out." I sipped the coffee. "Hey, you know this stuff is good." I sat back down.

We looked at each other. It was an awful moment, a shattered moment in which I heard things breaking and tearing. "You want confession, I'm available. In less than an hour in my booth at St. Hedwig's."

"You think I'm nuts?" I grinned at him. "There are some things I'd like to keep from you, Kev. You think I want you knowing everything about me?"

He saw through my feigned cheerfulness. He sat studying me, and I could tell he was trying to figure out how heavily I was into lying at the moment. And in what direction.

"So what are you gonna do, huh? You gonna go to Dad for me?" I stayed cheerful. I was even a little sassy. He was getting too close to seeing the truth, and I had to keep it from him, the truth being that I was a complete shattered mess and that with a little more urging on his part, I'd spill everything out to him.

"I don't know if I can. What defense can I come up with?"

"Just tell him what he's doing is cruel and unusual punishment. And that if he'd let up, maybe I'd come around. And that this isn't a contest of wills. He listens to everything you say."

"I can't, Brieanna. Precisely because he listens to

everything I say. I can't lie to him."

"That's not a lie."

"All right, I'll buy the part that it isn't a contest of wills. But that's all I can tell him. I have nothing to bargain with. You haven't given me anything."

"Couldn't you just go out on a limb for me, Kev? This time?"

"You sound as if I've never gone out on a limb for you before. This is one time I can't, Brie. You're putting me in a spot."

"Well, I will work things out if he gives me some room. The way it is now, I'm suffocating."

"You're doing penance. It won't hurt you to do penance once in a while. It doesn't hurt any of us. Brieanna, it's what you're hiding from me that I worry about. You're in some kind of trouble. I don't think you should be running free. I think I agree with Dad's method right now. Things don't look so good from where I sit. I'm sorry."

Sorry! That galled me. It just did. "Well, things don't look so good from where I sit either, Kevin McQuade."

"Let's not have this disintegrate into another fight."

"Just what I saw in here with Diana a few minutes ago didn't look so good to me."

"Brieanna, I can handle my own affairs, believe me."

"That's a poor choice of words, Kev."

The pupils of his eyes dilated. "That's a lousy remark, and I think you should take it back."

"I won't."

"Well, it's a rotten remark. And unworthy of you."

"You're in more trouble than I'm in, Kev."

"I can handle it if I am."

"No you can't. Because you're too stubborn and proud. Because you're Irish."

"Brieanna, get lost. You're sore because I won't plead your case with Dad. Now I don't wanna fight with you. So go. I can handle my relationship with Diana."

He gave me a steadfast look, right in the eyes. I knew what was behind the look. Irish determination. The kind they have when they go on hunger strikes in Ireland.

"You're a priest. You're not supposed to have relationships with women." I knew I was out of line even talking to him like that. It would make him angry. And I knew that as much as he loved me, he wouldn't hold that anger back. Maybe because he loved me.

"Brieanna, go." That was all he said. He leaned back in the chair, picked a pencil up from the desk, and turned it around in his hands, looking at it.

"Kev—"

"Out," he pointed to the door. "I'm getting really ticked off at you."

"I just said—"   .

"I know what you just said. Diana is a social worker. She has legitimate business here. What do you want me to do, kick her out? My bishop wouldn't ask me to do that."

"Your bishop doesn't see the way she looks at you." I held my breath, half expecting him to get up and usher me to the door personally. I wouldn't have been surprised if he'd done that. What he did do surprised me more, though. He started to speak, thought better of it, then slumped in the chair. "My bishop wouldn't even tell me what to do about Manuel. That's what I'm really in trouble over. That's the reason I look like I do. If I ever leave the priesthood, it will be because of the Manuels and not the Dianas."

What had he said? Leave the priesthood? My head shot up. "What?"

"You heard me."

Leave the priesthood, he'd said. Everything fell inside me. "You're *leaving*?"

"I said, *if* I ever do."

"Manuel," I croaked. "The guy who came to the door that day and left the letter for you?"

"The very same."

"What's with him?"

"Dad didn't tell you? Where you been all week? The whole town knows about me and Manuel."

"I've been in in-school suspension."

"He belongs to the Unification Church."

"You mean he's a Moonie?"

"I mean he's a very nice person. And my friend, from Newark. Last spring when I was down on funds, he came through so I could feed some poor families. His church came through. We became friends."

"You and a Moonie?" I was flabbergasted, but then why? Kev took up with all kinds of people in Newark.

"Brieanna, he's a very nice person. Anyway, the Unification Church is establishing itself in this town as part of an all-out effort in the state to be accepted. They've been having meetings in every county, inviting the clergy to come. It's something about uniting against Communism. Manuel was transferred here during the summer to establish a foothold in Waltham. He needed a place for his meeting. He had the clergy from all over the county invited. The Baptists promised him a hall and pulled out at the last minute. So he came to me. I promised him St. Hedwig's hall."

"You and a Moonie," I said again.

"Well, the Presbyterians found out about it. And the Methodists. I got calls. Was I crazy, aligning myself with a Moonie? Did I know what I was doing? I think one of them tipped off Dad's paper, because a reporter called and asked if it was true that I was giving St. Hedwig's to the Moonies."

"So what did you do?"

"Well"—and he grinned, putting me more at ease—"by then my bishop knew about it. He called me in. I have a good relationship with him. He didn't ask me to do anything. But I knew what I had to do. All I needed was a story in the press."

"Couldn't you have asked Dad to call off his reporter?"

He waved a hand. "You know better than that. I said no to Manuel. He had to call off his meeting."

I hesitated a moment, figuring. I could see how bad he felt even talking about this. But why? "You can't solve everybody's problems, Kev."

"Brieanna, I'm a priest. I'm supposed to be a good Christian. That means loving everybody. Now you tell me how I can turn Manuel away and be a good priest. That's my real problem. Not Diana. They told me in the seminary how to handle the Dianas. They never told me how to handle the Manuels."

"That's a bummer, Kev."

"What kind of a Christian am I?" he persisted. Oh, he was being hard on himself.

"You're always helping *everybody*, Kev."

He shook his head. "Not good enough. Manuel is in a heap of trouble with his superiors because of me. I haven't slept in a week. That's why I look as I do. Now you know my real problem."

"I shouldn't have bugged you."

"Don't be ridiculous." He stood up. I got up too. I moved to the door, my head spinning, trying to piece it all together. *Leave the priesthood!* The words were branded in fire on my brain. I stole a look at him. He smiled serenely. "I wish you would have let me help you today," he said.

His hand was on my shoulder. I felt the gentle

pressure of it. "Kev, you wouldn't really leave, would you?"

He smiled, and I felt as if I'd just come home again after a long absence. "I'm gonna be around for a while to keep after you. Don't look so devastated. Priests have doubts all the time. I'm coming late to mine, that's all. I'm tired. I'll be fine. Only I can't go to Dad on your behalf. I think you need to be confined right now. You need some quiet time to think."

"'S'okay, Kev."

"Come to me in a week. Or sooner, if you're ready. I'll have another shot at helping you. Any way you want to do it."

He meant it. I felt a glow of warmth inside. My resistance was melting too. Standing close to him, the pungent fragrance of his cassock, the mixture of incense and mustiness, almost made me dizzy with nostalgia for the safe world of my childhood that he had always represented. I knew that if I didn't get away from him, out of the circle of his arm, the pressure of his hand on my shoulder, I'd be spilling my guts out to him in two minutes.

Bless me, Father, for I have sinned. I'm an accomplice in hiding some drugs. I moved away. He let me go. I said something bright and sweet and went out the door and down the hall. I almost ran down that hall. The pressure of his hand on my shoulder stayed with me all the way home.

Chapter 12

Okay, that was it. No sense in thinking Kev could help me. He had his own problems. So there we were, Kev with his troubles and me with mine. And both of us too stubborn to confide in the other, both willful, and beset and tortured by our individual demons.

I felt more depressed than ever when I got home. Kev and I wore each other out. We worked on each other, gnawing away until we were both exhausted. I ran upstairs to my room, avoiding Alma as she came out of the kitchen to ask where I'd been. I threw myself on my bed.

I was going to have to stay away from Kev. He saw through me too easily. And I felt myself weakening and wanting to tell him everything. There was something about him. He could talk about leaving the priesthood all he wanted. But he had a charm, a

139

magic about him that melted all my resolve. He made it so easy to confide in him. And if I did, then what?

If I told him as my brother, then he, too, would be an accessory to a crime, to harboring drugs. He'd be obligated to do something about it, and if I knew Kev, what he'd do would be go with me to the authorities. If I went to him in confession, he wouldn't be able to tell, but he might wring promises from me that I couldn't keep. I didn't want to buy my freedom back that way. The price was too high.

I was worried about him, though. That business with Manuel really had him down. I'd never seen him so deflated and unsure. And no matter what he said about Diana not being the problem, I was sure she had something to do with his misery.

I don't know how long I lay there with all that stuff buzzing around in my head. I heard Dad's car come in the drive, heard him, a few minutes later, talking downstairs with Alma. Then he came upstairs, went into his room down the hall for a while. Shortly after that, there was a knock on my door and he came in.

"You all right, Brie?"

"Yeah."

"Well, come on down for supper. I'm going out later and I'm hungry."

I sat up on the bed. It was getting darker earlier now, and in the duskiness of my room, I saw my father leaning against the doorjamb. "You fight with Kev again?" he asked.

"No."

"All right. Why don't you wash up?"

"Daddy."

He'd turned to go. He stopped.

"Daddy, Kev's in trouble."

"I'm aware of that, Brie."

"Couldn't you ask your reporter not to write the story if Kev gives Manuel the hall?"

He sighed and looked at me. "First, Kev's already said no to Manuel. Second, I could but I won't. You know I don't run my newspaper that way."

"Don't you care about Kev?"

"Yes. But he went into it with his eyes open. He should have known better."

"He says he's being a Christian."

"I know what he says."

I stared at him accusingly, not quite believing what was coming out of him. I guess I never would really understand my father. One minute he was defending Kev, and the next he was just about saying Kev deserved what he got. "He says," I enunciated clearly, "that he doesn't know how he can be a good Christian when he has to break his promise to Manuel. Daddy, you know what I think? I think he's having doubts."

"It's about time," he said quietly. "We all have doubts. Who does he think he is not having them? Look, Brie, I know you think I sound heartless, but the one thing we all have to learn in life is what commitment really is. Kev may think he's committed to his priesthood, but he won't really find out until he's disillusioned. Commitment after disillusionment, that's the way it has to be if you're really going to cut it with anything that's important to you. Anybody can perform when the times are good and everything's with us. When you're riding on the tail wind of idealism. Try holding on to what you believe in when they pull the rug out from under you. That's when you know if you can cut the mustard. Kev's really never been tested in his priesthood, honey. One of these days, he will be. That's when he'll prove himself a really good priest."

I sat on the edge of my bed unable to say anything. Commitment after disillusionment. What did those words mean?

"You don't understand me," he said. "Do you?"

I shrugged.

"Look," he said. "Do you know how many times I wanted to quit the paper? How many times I got disillusioned? Not only since I've owned my own paper, but before, when I was working for somebody else. Newspapering isn't any easier than being a priest. It's in the same ballpark. You have to deal with people, listen to them, to their troubles, their stories. They come to you when they have no place else to go. You have to take their word on things, then put yourself on the line and write about them. Sometimes the person you trusted was lying, and there you are in print with egg all over your face. Some people tell you things, then decide, when they see their own words in print, that they can't stand it, and they accuse you of misquoting. Sometimes we spend weeks pursuing a public-service story, and the public doesn't give a damn, but leave out the cross-word puzzle and they scream."

He stopped. I just sat looking at him. It was getting darker in the room, so that I couldn't see the expression on his face anymore. His voice got softer. "And what about when your mother walked off on me. You think I didn't want to throw in the towel then?"

"I understand, Daddy," I said. I didn't, really, but I felt I ought to say something to him after that last admission. Simply because I knew how difficult it was for him to say it.

"All right, come on then." His voice was husky. "I'm hungry."

"I'm not, Daddy. Can't I be excused tonight?"

"No, you can't. You don't have to eat, but I want you at the table."

I got up and followed him. "Where are you going tonight?"

"We're going to a concert in Philadelphia. I want you in bed on time. I got you a movie from the video store."

"What'd you get?"

"The one you asked for. *Back to the Future*."

"Oh, neat." I'd asked for it before all the trouble on the island. I had no desire to see it anymore. All I wanted to do tonight was see Josh. The night loomed long and desolate before me. Alma would be doing her knitting in her room, watching television. The house would be quiet, and I'd wander from room to room like a prisoner in the exercise yard.

"The movie has to be back tomorrow before five," he was saying. "Or we pay extra. Remind me. And don't make all kinds of noise in the morning. I'll be wanting to sleep for a while. If I don't wake up for church, you'll have to go by yourself."

"Couldn't I go to church with Alma? I like her church, and she said I could go with her anytime I wanted."

"No, you should go to your own church. I don't mind your going with Alma once in a while, but you know your brother gets on me when you miss mass."

"But they sing the best gospel music at Shiloh Baptist."

"We're Catholic, Brie, not Baptist."

"And they don't have confession there. I think confession's dumb. Telling all your sins to another person. Do you think I'd ever tell my sins to Kev just because he's a priest?"

"Nobody asked you to. But you can take up those theological questions with him. I can't think on an empty stomach."

I never saw *Back to the Future* that night. I went out with Josh. I sneaked out without anybody knowing. I'd never done anything like that before, but I was finding out that I had the capability of doing lots of things I'd never done before. I knew that once

Alma went to sleep, nothing short of *Air Force One* landing in our backyard would wake her. And I knew that my dad would be home late. I didn't plan on sneaking out. It just happened.

Josh called around eight. My father had already left for his date with Amanda, looking nothing less than foxy in his tux. It was some kind of concert that required formal wear, and they were going out with friends afterward.

"Hi." Josh's voice was low and intimate on the phone, cutting through the October dark and touching chords inside me that brought tears to my eyes. "What are you doin'?"

"What do you think I'm doing? Sitting here in my room feeling sorry for myself."

"Hey"—and he laughed—"wha'd ya do all day?"

"I went to see Kev. Hoping he would talk to my dad and get him to take some of my chains off. But Kev wouldn't do it."

"What made you think he would?"

"Sometimes he talks to Dad for me when I need it. But this time he said no. He says I'm in some kind of trouble, and I need quiet time."

"Well, he's right about the first thing. I don't know about the second."

"I know he's wrong about that. I wanna see you, Josh."

"Hey, I wanna see you too. So stop it. You're only torturing yourself."

"Maybe you could come over. Dad won't be home

until late, and Alma goes to bed by nine. Last night was her night out, so she'll be tired. They had some big party at her church yesterday, and she worked all day there. Once she goes to sleep, she doesn't hear a thing. So you could come over."

"No way. I'm not gonna get caught sneaking around your house when I'm not supposed to be there. I don't think we should, Brie."

"I thought you said you wanted to see me."

"I *do!*" His voice croaked in indignation. "What do you think?"

"I think you're probably gonna go out tonight, that's what I think."

"Sure I am. I'm going to the refuge. Nothing else to do. And I want to see how Confucius is making out."

"Ohhh, Josh. I'd love to go there with you."

"Yeah, well I'd love to have you, sweetie, but I don't make the rules."

"You could come by and pick me up."

"Brie," he said warningly.

"We could sneak out the window."

"We?"

"I mean me. I could."

"Look, Brie, your old man would kill us. I mean, he's a nice guy and all, and up to now he's been pretty decent to me. But I know when to quit."

"He doesn't have to find out. Just for a couple of hours, okay? Who would know?"

"You gonna slip something into Alma's tea? No thanks."

"I can go out the window. I've got this big tree right outside my window, and the branches are easy to climb down. I know I could do it."

He hesitated as if he were actually considering the possibilities. I waited. "You ever done it before?" he asked. "Climb down the tree, I mean?"

"Well, no, but I could." I didn't elaborate and tell him how frightened I was of heights. Everybody in my family knew that. I think it all started the time Kev put me on top of that ladder. He traumatized me, that's what he did. I never got over it. So it would be at considerable personal sacrifice that I would climb down the maple tree outside my window. But it could be done, I was sure of it.

"You'll get hurt. A busted head, Brie," Josh was saying. "You better not. No, absolutely not. I've decided I want nothing to do with it."

"Joshua Falcone," I said with great dignity, "if you don't come over and pick me up, I'll do it anyway. I'll climb out the window and down the tree. I'll go out all alone. I don't know where I'll go, but I'll go somewhere. And if you don't come over and help me get down the tree, you'll be responsible if I fall."

"Do you think Romeo and Juliet really started like this?" Josh was saying. He stood at the base of the maple tree outside my window, talking to me while I inched my way down. It was very dark, with only the distant glow of streetlights from way across the lawn. Josh had parked his car on the side of the house, the side where I was climbing down. I wore jeans and a bulky knit sweater and sneakers for good traction, and I was edging my way bravely from one branch to another.

"I should have brought a safety net," he said.

I said nothing. The ground and Josh's voice were too far below for me to even open my eyes. I had climbed down two branches already and there was no going back up. I was stuck. Josh was talking to me, and I wasn't answering. My eyes were closed tightly, and I felt the fear rising inside my chest.

"Brie," he whispered urgently. "You okay?"

"I'm stuck."

"How? You caught on something?"

Sure I was caught on something. I was caught on the fear Kevin had instilled in me when I was a kid on that ladder. I was impaled on it.

"Brie?"

When I didn't answer, he started shimmying up the base of the tree. "Stay right where you are," he directed. "I'm coming."

I don't know what he intended to do or what I expected him to to, but I clung to the branch, waiting while I heard him inching closer and closer. "All right, Brie, I'm right behind you." He touched my leg. "You were doing great, I don't know why you stopped. Now just keep holding on and sliding down. I'm right behind you. If you start to fall, I'll grab you. Come on."

He talked me down that tree, urging me inch by inch, until we got to a lower branch. "We can jump now, Brie, if you want," he suggested. "Here, I'll go first. Watch."

I didn't watch. I screwed my eyes shut again, but he made the jump in a second. I looked down to see the ground about eight feet below me, and Josh standing there holding up his arms.

"Come on, I'll catch you. Hey, you can't stay there all night."

I jumped. Josh tried to catch me, but all I did was knock him over. He grabbed for me, missed, and clipped the side of my face with his elbow as we both went down. I landed the wrong way on one ankle. And we lay there in the dry leaves laughing and moaning and shushing each other. When I got up, I didn't feel anything right off, but as the night went on, I began to realize that I must have sprained my ankle. And the bruise up near my eye hurt like any-thing.

But it was worth it. Once inside Josh's car, I felt as if I'd escaped from prison. The night was heavenly, crisp and clear, with the air like silk.

"Oh, Josh, look!"

A great round moon was rising over the trees. There wouldn't be many more nights like this. "C'mon," Josh said, "I've got to have you back before the witching hour."

* * *

The moon was shining like a great yellow balloon in the sky by the time we drove up the hill to the refuge. It was absolutely eerie at night, that place. The beige stucco buildings of the prison stood out in the moonlight, and the barbed wire on top of the fence in the exercise yard gleamed like silver.

"We can't get inside the building at night," Josh explained. "I could if I had to, since I have a key. But they don't like it unless it's absolutely necessary. So we'll go into the yard."

He took me around the side of the main building to a fenced-in area. "This is where most of the animals are kept," he whispered. And he unhooked the large wooden gate.

It was as if we were in another world. The prison buildings loomed behind us, and above us was the full yellow moon shining down and reflecting off a small pool of water in the distance. I sensed the presence of *things*, of creatures, but I could not see any. Straight ahead was the huge flight cage where I knew Confucius was, and I could hear the beating of his wings as he flew around inside, since owls are nocturnal. But then I heard more rustlings of wings to the right, and instinctively I stepped closer to Josh.

"Those are the crows," he said. "Come say hello."

The cage was about six by eight and a good fifteen feet high. Inside were a lot of tree branches growing out of the ground and on them perched four crows. One of them came right up to the wire mesh of the cage and cocked his head sideways, looking at us.

"This is Sinbad," Josh said, reaching in between the mesh of the cage and scratching his head. "He likes that, don't you, fella?"

"Oh, he's darling! Can I pet him?"

"Sure."

"But his beak is so long! Will he bite me?"

"Of course not, he's dying for attention. He only has one wing, see? He can't fly, but he loves people. He's become a real pet. He's the friendliest of all of them."

The other three crows were regarding me cautiously from branches at the far end of the cage, but Sinbad blinked his beady eye at me and moved his head as I scratched him. I had never seen a crow up so close before. "Oh Josh, I feel so bad for him that he can't ever fly again!"

"Yeah, well, he's adjusted. Better than some humans do to certain situations," Josh said philosophically. "Come on, you wanna see Madame Pompadour?"

I followed him to a low hutchlike creation. Josh squatted down and unhooked the door, urging whatever was inside to come out. In a few minutes, a hairy *thing* emerged, nose first. "This is Madame Pompadour, the skunk," he said solemnly.

I backed off instantly, and he laughed. "Hey, she's de-skunked. They make great pets. Of course, there is some residue of odor but still..."

Tentatively, I reached out and petted her. "They

don't live very long," Josh explained. "Only about six years, and she's around five. Someone had her since she was a baby and moved and couldn't keep her anymore. She'll stay here now."

From the skunk, we went to the raccoon with its adorable masked face, and Josh explained to me how this was the one he'd bottle-fed last spring, and they would soon be taking it into the wild to run free again. There were pigeons, an opossum, squirrels that had been brought in when they were so tiny that they'd had to be kept in an incubator, and geese around the small pool.

"The geese come in wounded," Josh explained. "Most of the time from one of the local golf courses. We've let many of them go for the summer, but in the fall, they'll be brought in again. They can all walk, but they'll never fly."

"What are the white ones?"

"Pekin ducks."

"Oh, I love the way they lay with their heads twisted around and resting on their backs. No rabbits?"

"No. The crop brought in during the spring have all been let go. Rabbits grow up very quickly," Josh explained. "In a few short weeks, they're ready to be on their own. When rabbits are born they have a white spot on top of their heads. We know they're ready to be on their own when that white spot disappears."

"Josh, you know so much about wildlife." I

stopped and looked up at him in the middle of the animal compound. Overhead the moon was rising higher, it's yellow light turning white. In the distance, because we were so high up on the hill, I could see the river shining, a ribbon of light in the October night. Around us the leaves rustled soothingly on the trees. I wanted to stay there forever, I decided. It was peaceful with the animals. I didn't want to go back outside the gates of the compound. I didn't want to go home again and face all my problems. Kev and Diana, the drugs on the island, my ankle, which was hurting like the devil, and what my father would say when he saw the bruise on my eye in the morning.

"Thanks for bringing me, Josh," I said.

"Yeah. It's always nice here. Quiet. And the animals are so appreciative of any attention. Come on, we'll pay our respects to Confucius, and then I guess we'd better get going."

My ankle hurt through most of the night. Josh had climbed up the tree with me again and helped me in the window. Once inside, I knelt on the floor, and our faces were so close as I looked out at him that I was sure he was going to kiss me. But he didn't. He just touched the bruise on my eye tenderly. "You better take a hot shower," he said, "and get some sleep. Is the ankle bad?"

"It'll be okay."

"I'll call you tomorrow."

"It was great, Josh. It was the most fun ever. I love sharing the animals with you."

"Well, since we're partners in crime, I figure we might as well be partners in something nice too," he said. "Hey, I better go, it's late."

I fell asleep between waves of pain in my ankle and dreamed of Josh and me flying through the night like Peter Pan and Wendy along with Sinbad, who somehow managed to fly despite only having one wing.

I slept late. By the time I got up in the morning, my father was already at breakfast. Alma had left for church and she had our food on the sideboard in warming pans. Scrambled eggs and home fries and sausage and muffins. I hobbled over to fill my plate.

My father looked up from his morning paper. "What happened to you?"

My back was to him as I served myself. "I came downstairs to get a snack last night and fell down some steps. I just slipped."

When I turned around, he was looking at me, paying particular interest to the bruise on the corner of my eye. "You look as if you were in a fight."

"I hit my head on the banister, Daddy."

"Didn't you wake Alma and tell her?"

"I didn't want to bother her." I was getting so good at lying. I was able to let the lies trip off my tongue with no pangs of conscience at all anymore. This morning I didn't care. Even though I was hurting, I was filled with a sense of warm satisfaction from my jaunt with Josh last night. We had shared something beautiful, something nobody else knew about. And the fact that I had sneaked out to do it only gave it another dimension of delight. So nothing could touch me this morning, I was sure of it.

"Here." My father pulled out my chair and took my plate from me as I sat down. Then he put his hand under my chin and turned my face to him. "Why didn't you put some ice on your face at least? People will accuse me of child abuse. Look, I think you'd better eat, and then we'll get over to the emergency room. That ankle needs attention."

"I'll be okay, Daddy."

"I told you about those slippers on the stairs," he said. "I told you they have no traction and you'd go flying someday, didn't I?"

"Yes, Daddy, you told me."

"We go to the emergency room after breakfast," he said. "No arguments. I was wondering why you were sleeping so late. I had Alma look in on you, but she said you were sleeping soundly and she didn't want to disturb you. Well, you missed mass again. I hope you're ready to do the explaining to your brother when he asks you why."

Kev came for Sunday dinner. I was on the chair in the living room with my ankle taped up, resting it on the ottoman, when he wandered into the room with a pre-dinner cocktail in hand. Alma and Daddy and Amanda were in the kitchen. Alma was carrying on about how useless she felt by not waking up last night when I fell.

"That child must have made some noise when she took that fall. How could I have slept through it? My room is right down the hall."

Amanda was telling her not to blame herself. They didn't expect her to lie awake nights listening for noises. And my father said I had no right to be wandering around the house at night anyway.

Kev stood there looking at me. "So you took a header."

I looked up. "Yeah, Kev."

"The way you run up and down those steps two at a time. You've been flying up and down those steps since you were four years old."

"Well, maybe it's because I didn't put the light on last night."

"You can take those steps with your eyes shut and one hand taped behind your back," he insisted.

I looked at him. And I saw the blue eyes observing me in that piercing way he had. For a minute neither of us said anything. The blue eyes were as cold as granite. But there was a glint of amusement in them too.

"I missed you in church this morning," he said.

"Yeah, I'm sorry, Kev. I guess I just slept late. I took some aspirin for the pain in my ankle, and once I did get to sleep, I just didn't wake up."

He nodded. "I'm wondering if missing mass is the

worst thing you've done in the last twenty-four hours."

My head shot up. I laughed. "Kev! Whatever are you saying?"

"You know what I'm saying." But before I could argue anymore, he turned and walked out. There was nothing I could have said anyway. Any further protest of mine would only make it worse. Because Kev knew the truth. At least Kev knew that I was lying.

Chapter 13

Oddly, things improved considerably after that. My dad realized I was hurt, for one thing, and decided he would drive me to school every day. But how would I get home? Kev was too busy, and Alma didn't drive anymore since she had an accident last year.

"Josh could drive me home, Dad," I said.

That was difficult for him. Because it was important for him to hold his ground with me. He did not like losing ground ever, with anybody.

His whole career as a newspaperman was based on the fact that every day of his life he dug in and held his ground, even on small matters. But there wasn't much he could do now and so he compromised.

"Josh can drive you home from school. And that's all. You're still grounded, just the same as before. What time does school let out?"

"Quarter of three, Daddy."

"Then you're to be home and in the house by three o'clock. Josh is not to come in with you. He only drives you home from school. Is that clear?"

"Yes, Daddy."

My life was picking up. At least Josh and I would have those fifteen minutes together every day. All I had to do now was make the injured ankle last a couple of weeks. In-school suspension lasted one more week, and then I was back on my regular schedule. I got excused from gym because of my ankle, and since Josh had that period free, we met in the *Close Call* office. He helped me with my work, because I had credits to make up.

He was really good in geometry and history. At Chittendon, before he'd gotten into trouble, he was straight-A. And we worked well together. Sure, there were other kids in the office working on the paper, but as far as I was concerned, there wasn't anybody else in the world.

I saw no reason to mention these sessions to my father. It was wrong, of course, that I couldn't, because without Josh's help, I probably wouldn't have made up my lost credits. Josh was tutoring me, is what he was doing. For nothing. But I knew Dad wouldn't buy that story. When you thought about it, of course, I saw no reason why he should. I'd been doing nothing but lying my head off to him for weeks now. Why should he believe me about anything?

Before long, Josh and I were inseparable in school. We were what they called an item. Nobody thought anything of it. Plenty of kids were going steady, and the only rule old Randolph had was that there were to be no public displays of affection in school or on the grounds.

He didn't have to waste his time worrying about that, not with Josh and me. There weren't even any private displays of affection. It just didn't happen.

I kept telling myself it didn't matter, of course, that Josh Falcone, the most handsome and considerate boy I ever met, never made a pass at me. The days just went on into weeks. We snuck out every Saturday night.

"You feel like climbing down any trees this Saturday?" he'd ask me. And I'd say yes. But then he'd look at me and shake his head. "We shouldn't. I shouldn't be encouraging you. We could get into a lot of trouble if your dad finds out."

Even the idea of getting into a lot of trouble with Josh intrigued me. "We've already done enough to get into trouble," I'd remind him. He knew what I meant. We were irrevocably bound together by the drugs on the island.

"There is nothing like a shared misery to hold people together," Alma had often told me. Well, Josh and I shared a misery all right. We often talked about the drugs in whispered tones.

"I've been monitoring Buetell," Josh told me one fine day in mid-October. "He's sold a lot of the stuff off already. He's been making regular fishing trips to the island. He said the fishing is pretty good there."

And that's the way Josh would keep me informed
about what was happening with Buetell and the
drugs. "The fishing was pretty good over the weekend," he'd tell me in school on Monday.

That meant Buetell was selling off the stuff. I was
overridden with guilt about all of it, of course. Most
of the time I put it out of my mind. Who was Buetell
selling the drugs to? Kids in school? I didn't want to
know. Of course, the kids in school who did drugs
would get their supply from somewhere if not from
Buetell. You could rationalize it that way. But I knew
better than that. I knew I was wrong. I knew sin
when I saw it. And I couldn't absolve myself of par-
ticipation in this sin no matter how I tried.

Going out with Josh on Saturday nights was the
only thing that kept me sane while my father still imposed his sentence upon me. I wasn't allowed to see
friends. I wasn't allowed to just ride around town on
my bike without asking Dad's permission. I wasn't
even permitted to go over to Second Chance without
Dad's special dispensation.

So I looked forward to my Saturday nights, hoping
Dad would always be out. And he was. We went,
every Saturday night, to the refuge, of course. I got to
know all the animals. I watched Confucius in the
flight cage, I stood by while Josh fed him mice. I got
to know Madame Pompadour and the opossum and
the squirrels and the geese, every one of them around
the little pool. I established a real friendship with
Sinbad the crow. And in the October nights, with the

leaves rustling in the distance and the shared love of the animals, Josh and I developed an intimacy, a closeness that was almost mystical.

On the third Saturday night, we were watching Confucius fly back and forth in his huge cage when Josh started to talk about Chittendon.

He missed it, he said. "This school can't hold a candle to it, Brie. The academic standards there are much higher. And there's more order. The kids all have a sense of purpose. Here so many of them are just putting in time."

I listened, afraid to break the spell when he started talking about Chittendon, because he never really opened up about it before. I could sense his pain, because the words came slowly, hesitantly.

"They didn't really kick me out, you know. The colonel said that he would have to, but I could resign first. So I did."

"On account of what happened with his daughter?"

"Yeah. When he found out what happened with us, he was sore, sure. He gave me this big long lecture, telling me how betrayed he felt and how I had not acted with honor and how I had gone against everything taught at the school. But he was more disappointed, I think, to find out what his daughter was. That's when he told me I could resign. So I did. It was the only thing to do."

I didn't push him about Chittendon, and I think he appreciated that.

Another Saturday night, we stood for a long time

under the maple tree outside my window, talking. It was cold and I shivered, longing for Josh to take me in his arms, for by now I was very much in love. I wanted him to hold me and kiss me.

"You go up first, Juliet," he said, hoisting me into the tree.

"Why did you call me that?" I sat where the limbs converged, looking at him.

"It fits, don't you think?"

"They had an unhappy ending."

He shrugged, huddling in his jacket. "They were the first of the teenage suicides. Ahead of their time. Today, it's a real social issue."

"They were lovers," I insisted.

"Well, they shouldn't have been. They were too young. Trouble is they had no teen athletic programs in those days. No high school newspapers. If they did, who knows? Romeo might have been star of the field hockey team. Juliet might have been a reporter for the high school paper."

"Josh, you have no romance in your soul."

"You'd better get up that tree before your old man gets home. I don't think he's got much romance in his, either. I'll stay here until you're inside."

Why did he date me? Why did he bother? I was starting to ask myself some very necessary questions.

Could I believe what he said about Chittendon? That having gotten sexually involved with a girl, he was determined it would never happen again? That he just wanted friendship? I knew how much he missed the military school, how he was paying for his sin. Still, maybe it was me. Maybe I just wasn't sexy enough. Kev had said I would break a lot of hearts by the time I was eighteen. I didn't want to break hearts.

All I wanted was for Josh to kiss me.

I woke up late the next morning, Sunday, as I'd been doing every Sunday morning for the last month or so. I was supposed to get myself off to church, of course, but I didn't. I just didn't have the heart for it. For one thing, I was convinced that I was so full of sin, between my complicity over the drugs at the island and my physical urges for Josh, that it didn't matter whether I went to church or not. Certainly, I couldn't go to communion without going to confession, and I couldn't go to confession without telling a priest about the drugs. So missing mass was just one more sin at this point, and I didn't really think it mattered.

I took my time getting up, and dressed. I examined myself in the mirror. It was my figure that was the problem, I decided. I just didn't have the right equipment. My breasts were too small. Amanda had always told me that I had a nice build, that I was just right and would be glad of it when I was forty.

I didn't care about the problems of being forty. I would gladly endure being overweight and sagging then, if only I were more generously endowed now. I was convinced, by the time I went down to breakfast, that it was because I didn't fill my clothes properly that Josh didn't get turned on by me. Maybe I would get a push-up bra, the kind with the wire under the cups.

Only Alma was in the kitchen, preparing Sunday breakfast. She was off to church soon. Her church lasted for hours, one reason I was glad I wasn't Baptist. I watched her whipping up some pancake batter. I was wearing my jeans and sweatshirt, with nothing on my feet.

"Go get something on your feet," she directed. "You'll catch cold."

"Alma, can I ask you a question?"

She had on her good blue dress and her hat with the silk flowers. Her good navy blue coat and white gloves were on a nearby chair. Her round black face cast me a knowing look. "Ask."

"Do you think there's a possibility that someday soon I'll start to look sexy?"

She sighed wearily. "I figured something was wrong with you these days."

"Alma, please, do you?"

"I certainly hope not. You're giving your daddy enough grief now."

"I'm tired of waiting. All the girls in school have good figures. I just about fit into a thirty-two A bra."

"Good Lord, child. Children are starving in Africa."

"Alma, they'd still be hungry even if I grew into a thirty-four B."

She grunted and carried the bowl of pancake mix to the refrigerator. "Seems to me you've got enough," she said.

"Enough for what? I'm skinny."

"What are you planning on doing that you need this terrific figure for? Entering the Miss America contest?"

"The boys don't pay any attention to me."

"Child, you've got the nicest boy driving you home every day since you hurt your ankle. What more do you want?"

"I want to be taken seriously."

"You don't have to wear thirty-four B for that."

"Yes I do. That's what boys like."

She scowled. "Don't you let your daddy hear you talk like that. Or Father Kevin. Child, you're a woman already. You're built like your mama. She was dainty like you. She was a dancer at one time, remember. You don't want to be buxom. That's not beautiful."

"Men think so."

"Your daddy didn't. He loved your mama just the way she was. For a long time before she left and for too long after. Love has nothing to do with dimensions. You can't measure love."

Alma had a way of doing that, putting something into terms I couldn't argue with. How could I argue with my parents' onetime love for each other? She knew I couldn't handle that. She wiped her hands on her apron and took it off. "Whatever's gotten into you lately, Brieanna McQuade, I don't know. You're smarter than that. And you're so pretty. You have beautiful hair and good bone structure, good skin and teeth. You're just lovely, child."

"Oh, Alma, what good is *lovely!*"

"Don't' you let the Lord hear you talk like that." She picked up her pocketbook and coat and made for the door. "And speaking of the Lord, why aren't you dressed for church?"

"It's late, I've already missed the last mass," I said lamely.

Again she grunted. "Seems to me you've been doing an awful lot of that lately. Your daddy said you were to go to church this morning. I woke you in time."

"I know, Alma, don't scold. Please, I don't feel like going to church. I've been going through this awful time and nobody seems to care."

"You've been going through an awful time all right. Worrying about the size of your bosoms. When Father Kevin asks why you weren't at mass, you can tell *him* what's on your mind. See what *he* has to say." And with that she walked out, the silk flower on her hat shaking from her indignation.

Chapter 14

It was the week before Halloween. In school, there was an undercurrent of excitement as invitations for parties generated like brush fires all around me. The ground swell of concern was focused on costumes, of course. This was one holiday where ingenuity counted for more than money. A lot of kids had taken to going to the Second Hand Rose Shop in town, which had pretty good used clothes. I'd planned on doing that myself this year. I was through with the baby costumes Alma always put together for me and had been saving my allowance to buy a flapper dress from the twenties, maybe. Or a man's jacket and trousers and hat, to be Charlie Chaplin. The ultimate for me, I had decided, would be to get Kev's cassock. But the one time I even mentioned it to him, he scowled so fiercely that I realized I'd sunk to depths of decadence that even I wasn't aware of.

I wouldn't be going to any party anyway. What was the difference? I knew my dad wouldn't let up on me just for Halloween. As the week progressed, I got more and more depressed hearing all the secret giggles and whispered plans around me. Then, on Thursday, Josh came up as I was leaving school. My ankle was mended now, so he wasn't allowed to drive me home anymore, but we managed to see each other every day anyway.

"Guess what? I'm talking Mr. Stephens into allowing me to release Confucius on Halloween night. Friday."

"Ohhh, Josh! That's great! Oh, I want to be there."

"Could you get out?"

"I could. Alma's not even home on Friday nights. And Dad and Amanda have a Halloween party at the country club. I could walk out the front door! I wouldn't even have to go out the window."

He grinned. "We have a date then." I stood in the school hall as kids rushed past me, staring at Josh's retreating back. What a way to spend Halloween! Who, of all these kids in school with their elaborate plans for parties and costumes, would ever have the privilege of letting an owl loose to go back into the wild on Halloween night?

I was bursting with excitement. I could barely contain myself. The only fly in the ointment was that I had no one to share my joy with. I couldn't mention it to anyone who mattered. Then Thursday night at supper, my dad sat spooning his soup into his mouth and looking at me.

"Would you like to help out at the party at the country club on Halloween, Brie? They need extra hands. Somebody got the bright idea to hire high school students, but they're in short supply. It seems they're all tied up with their own parties. You'd be paid well."

I was too surprised to answer right away. All kinds of confusing thoughts merged in my head. Collided was the better word for it.

"Brie?" He was waiting for my answer. Well, he could wait! Here he had me under cruel and unusual punishment, still grounded for something I'd done over a month ago, and then he wanted me to go and help out at the club because they couldn't get the other high school kids.

"I've got a lot of studying to do this weekend, Daddy, to make up for the work I missed in in-school suspension," I said. Miraculously, I assembled my thoughts and sounded coherent.

He scowled. "You've been studying every weekend. You haven't caught up yet?"

"I lost a lot of credit, Daddy."

He nodded, saying nothing. And we didn't speak much during the rest of supper. But when it was over he looked at me. "I hope you're not getting back at your old dad because he punished you, Brie," he said sadly. "I hope you really do have studying Friday night."

I felt the tears misting in my eyes and choking back
any reply I could make. I shrugged, tried to speak,
and failed. Lucky for me, he interpreted the tears as
hurt instead of remorse.

"I'm sorry, honey," he said. "I know you'd help out
if you could. Forget what I just said. I didn't mean
it."

There was, as if on rush order, a full moon on Halloween. And a clear sky with only a few shredded
bits of clouds. I followed Josh and Mr. Stephens into
the animal compound. Mr. Stephens was a broad,
bearded man with the kindest eyes I'd ever seen. He
only smiled when Josh told him that I was supposed
to be helping out at the country club tonight. And he,
Josh, would greatly appreciate it if we could keep
quiet the fact that I had opted to come here instead.

"Don't blame you one bit," Mr. Stephens said to
me. "I'd rather be here than at a party at the country
club myself."

Confucius saw us coming and clucked in warning
as Mr. Stephens and Josh unlocked the flight cage
and went inside. Josh was wearing fireplace gloves
for protection from Confucius's talons. He also carried a towel. Acting on the soft-spoken directions
from Mr. Stephens, he approached Confucius in a far
corner of the flight cage and threw the towel over him
at exactly the right moment.

Then he picked him up by the shoulders, pinning
his wings. "That's it, Josh, you've got him," Mr. Ste-

phens was saying. "Hold on to him now by the shoulders and bring him here."

They knelt down, Confucius between them, and I saw the exerted effort on Josh's face as he held Confucius while Mr. Stephens used a pair of pliers to put a band on his leg.

"There you go, fellow," Mr. Stephens said. "Now you can turn up in South America, and anyone who spots you can call the information in to Laurel, Maryland. It'll go into a computer and help us to learn your migration habits."

"South America?" My voice cracked and I felt a rush of alarm. "He could fly all the way down there?"

"They've been known to." Mr. Stephens smiled up at me. "Wherever he goes, he's got the band on him so he can be tracked. Now bring him out into the yard, Josh. It's time."

Tenderly, as if he were carrying a baby, Josh held on to Confucius, who was still quiet under the towel. In the yard, Mr. Stephens removed the towel and Confucius became alert. "Now, just raise your arms, Josh, and let him go."

Josh hesitated for only a fraction of a second, and I could tell he was saying good-bye to Confucius. I was aware of the tears streaming down my own face as I thought of that owl leaving us, spreading his wings and taking off into the night. Where would he go? How would he know the way?

"Josh!" Mr. Stephens urged.

Then, as if in some well-rehearsed ballet, Josh raised his arms and, for a moment, seemed a part of Confucius. As the bird felt the movement, he raised his own wings and stood poised. Then, as if he was rushing off to some prearranged appointment, Confucius surged forward with a mighty thrust, his wing-spread stretching to full capacity, all his muscles straining, and took off.

We stood watching, the three of us, as he became part of the night. Upward and upward he flew. I thought my heart would burst inside watching him. Then he circled and headed for a group of tall trees in the distance where he landed, perched on an uppermost limb. We could barely see him.

"He'll be all right," Mr. Stephens said. "He's getting his bearings."

He seemed to be looking in our direction. "He's saying good-bye," Josh grinned.

"Let's go," Mr. Stephens suggested. "Let's not linger. I want him to go off on his own."

We started to leave the compound. As we reached the gate we heard, or rather sensed, the flutter of his wings and, turning, saw him flying off into the night.

Josh and I left the refuge and drove around for a while afterward, still feeling the exhilaration of what we'd done, what we'd been a part of.

"I've never had a Halloween like it," I said. "It's better than any party I've ever been to."

"It *was* a party," Josh said simply.

He took me to the only ice-cream stand that was still open outside town, and we celebrated over sundaes, eating them in his car and talking about Confucius. Then he took me home. It was only ten-thirty, but I didn't care. The night was complete. Nothing could add to it or detract from it. We didn't even have much to say to each other on the way home, but our silence was communal. We were on the same wavelength. We didn't need to speak.

At the front door, he kissed me. On the forehead. I was dumbstruck. I stood looking up at him and saw the look in his eyes, the apology, the pleading.

"Josh."

"Ssh. Be quiet. Go inside. " He took the key and opened the door. I went inside like a zombie, found my way upstairs, threw myself down on my bed, fully dressed, and went to sleep.

I dreamed about Josh and Confucius. I saw the great owl lifting off into the air, while Josh stood poised with his arms uplifted. In spite of the fact that Josh had only kissed me on the forehead, my happiness had reached its peak.

Saturday morning it rained and I slept late. I went downstairs to make my own breakfast because Alma wouldn't be back until afternoon. It wasn't bad. I wanted to be alone. The kitchen was cozy and lamplit. My dad was still sleeping upstairs, and I toasted bagels and had coffee. I was reading my dad's paper when a knock came on the back door.

It was Kevin. I let him in.

"Hi, Kev. " I had a mouth full of bagel.

"I've been up since five-thirty. Got any breakfast?"

"Sure. " I sat him down and gave him coffee and set about scrambling some eggs and frying some bacon. I was a fair-to-middling cook myself, since I'd had to make do many times when Alma wasn't around. In no time at all, we were seated at the kitchen table, eating.

"Dad still asleep?"

"Yeah. He and Amanda came in late from the club."

"Well, Manuel got a place for his meeting. Diana found him a hall."

"That's great, Kev. " I tried to sound enthusiastic.

"Yeah, well it doesn't let me off the hook with myself, though. How come you haven't been to mass, Brieanna?"

That brought me up short. "What?"

"Do you know what day this is?"

"It's Saturday."

"It's a holy day. November First. All Saints' Day. You weren't at mass. Of course, you haven't been at mass either Saturday night or on Sunday for weeks now."

"Gee, I forgot about today, Kev. Honest."

"Did you forget last Sunday too? And the three or four Sundays before that?"

"Hey, what is this?"

"Nothing. This isn't anything. When was the last

time you received the sacraments?"

I got annoyed. Here I was basking in the remnants of last night's once-in-a-lifetime experience, and he had to walk in and bring his harsh reality down on my head. "Is that why you're here?"

"No. I came for breakfast. You going to church somewhere else that I don't know about?"

"Are we gonna fight, Kev? 'Cause I don't feel like it."

"No reason to fight. " The blue eyes were placid. "I just thought there was something I could help you with. I told you to come to me again, so I could help you. You didn't. So I've come to you."

"I hurt my ankle. You know how hard it is to get around on crutches. That's why I couldn't get to mass."

"You've been off crutches for a couple of weeks now. " He smiled. "I can't remember the last time you came and knelt at the altar rail so I could give you communion. It always meant a lot to me to see you there."

I ducked my head and looked at my coffee. Sure I could say it was none of his business. But he'd made it his business a long time ago. It was too late to stop him now.

"Where were you last night, Brie?" he asked gently.

I raised my eyes to look at him.

"I called. " In the quiet lamp-lit kitchen his voice

sounded like velvet. "Dad said you were here study-ing. I called your number. I was going to ask you to come to mass Saturday night. There was no answer."

Tears came to my eyes. I just looked at him ap-pealingly.

"Don't worry, I'm not gonna say anything to Dad. But I'd like to know. I'm worried about you, Brieanna."

"I was out," I said.

The blue eyes absorbed that, adjusted to it. Care-ful, careful, I could hear him telling himself. Some-thing here. She's in trouble. His eyes sort of change color when you hit him head-on with something like that. They go from light blue to hazy gray.

"Where were you?"

"Where I've been every Saturday night for weeks. With Josh. I've been sneaking out. I go out the win-dow. Down the maple tree. Except for last night. Last night I went out the front door 'cause Alma wasn't here."

There. That'd keep him busy for a while if he wanted to worry about me. I felt glad, actually, at being able to tell him, at being able to tell somebody. I didn't know how much longer I was going to be able to keep all that bottled up inside me.

"You're afraid of heights. " That's what he said. That's what he remembered, of all things to say.

"You made me that way. You put me on a ladder once when I was a kid."

"That's how you hurt your ankle. I knew it was something like that. You told Dad you fell down the stairs."

I saw him forming things in his mind. "You sneak out the *window?* Where do you go?"

"Oh, Kev, it's so neat! We go to the wildlife refuge that the county runs up at the correctional center. Josh works there part-time. I mean he volunteers. I met all the animals. Sinbad, the crow with one wing. And Madame Pompadour, the skunk, and the squirrels and geese and opossum. And Confucius. He's the owl. He was so beautiful, Kev. And I've been going to see him every Saturday night with Josh. He was in the flight cage in the yard exercising his flight muscles so he could be let free. That's what we did last night. We let him go. He went back to the wild."

I stopped, my eyes glistening with the relish of telling it to somebody, finally.

"You know the trouble you'll be in if Dad finds out?"

"That's all you can say? Kev, I've just told you about the most wonderful things I've been doing, things I never would have seen if I didn't know Josh, and that's all you can say?"

"I'm happy you were doing such healthy and nice things, Brieanna," he said solemnly, "and I can see by your face how much it means to you. But honey, you've lost your perspective here a little bit. You're lying to Dad. You're disobeying him, and you're running around with a boy he's forbidden you to see. "

"I know all that."

"Well?"

"I thought *you* would understand. It's the only thing right now that's keeping me sane."

He nodded. "If Dad found out, he'd be awfully hurt, Brie. He's a good father to you. He deserves better."

"Well, I don't deserve to be punished like he's punishing me. And I can't stand it anymore." I glared at him defiantly. He nodded his head, saying nothing for a minute.

"Are you going to keep doing this? Sneaking out the window on Saturday nights?"

"As long as I have to, yes."

"I see hurt down the road for you, Brie. For you and Dad. I don't like it. I don't know if I like you running around at night with this boy when Dad doesn't even know you're out."

"Is that what you're worried about? His reputation? The things you've heard about him?"

"Well, I can't help *that*, Brie. He does have a reputation."

"You don't have to worry," I said. "He's never even made a pass at me."

"Well, he's decent then."

"He's never even kissed me."

"And that bothers you."

"Yeah, it bothers me. He was kicked out of Chittendon for fooling around with the colonel's daughter. He says he doesn't want to get involved with a girl again. But it's more than that."

"What more?" he asked carefully.

I felt everything relax inside me. It was good to be able to discuss things with somebody finally. I was almost grateful to Kev for being inquisitive. "I don't know. It all doesn't add up. The only thing I can think of is that I'm not sexy enough. I haven't got a good enough figure."

He kept a straight face. "You've got the figure," he said.

"You're my brother. What do you know?"

"I know you disappoint me. That's what I know. Because the only value you're placing on yourself comes from the eyes of a man."

I stared at him. He took out a cigarette and lit it. "What kind of a dumb thing is that to say?" I asked.

"Think about it. You're all bent out of shape, because this guy hasn't tried anything with you. You think you're worthless. That you're a failure."

"I didn't say that."

"You don't have to. It's written all over you. You're climbing out the window, risking life and limb and your reputation with Dad, to prove something to yourself. And you're not proving it. And you're miserable."

"I'm not miserable. I'm only wondering what's wrong with me."

"There's nothing wrong with you. He's taking you out, obviously sharing with you something that's very special in his life. Why can't you just be happy with that?"

"I am. But we've become pretty close, Kev. Don't you think he'd at least want to kiss me?"

He got up and walked across the kitchen to take his dishes to the sink. "Maybe he just wants to be friends. When I was dating in high school, the girls always liked going out with me because I didn't try anything. They said they didn't have to worry."

"Kev, you were gonna be a *priest!*"

"I wasn't a priest yet. I don't know, Brie. Maybe he just likes to be with you. Do you find that so hard to accept? Maybe he likes the way you climb trees. I do know one thing, though. This isn't the reason you haven't been coming to church or going to the sacraments, is it?"

"No."

He nodded. "I wish you'd tell me what's really wrong, Brie."

I didn't answer.

"I'd like to see you in church again. Father Peterson is always available for confession, and you know how easygoing he is. I'm gonna back off now, give you awhile longer. I just wanted to make sure you were all right. When Dad said you were home last night and I called and got no answer, I was worried."

He came over and kissed me on top of the head and put on his raincoat. "I don't approve of what you're doing, sneaking out like that. And I hope you don't

break a leg, and I hope, more than that, that Dad
doesn't catch you. But I'm glad to hear Josh is so
decent and that you've found some worthwhile activ-
ity to do together. Although I do wish you'd do it by
the light of day. " He grinned down at me. "Don't
worry, your secret is safe with me. In two weeks,
though, if you don't start coming to mass again and I
don't see you at the communion rail, I'm really gonna
conduct the Inquisition. You hear?"

I nodded, feeling the tears in the back of my
throat. I loved him an awful lot, I decided, watching
him walk across the kitchen. At the back door, he
paused and winked. "Do it for me, Brie. Come back
to church. I'd like to know I had some influence.
Nothing else seems to be working for me these days."

And in the next minute, he was gone, out into the
rain, leaving me with the feeling that he really meant
it.

Chapter 15

Things never work out the way you figure them to work in life. Or as Alma always put it, "The best laid plans of mice don't often take into consideration the cats."

It's the cats that get us all the time, Alma says. Meaning the things we don't count on happening. I never, for instance, counted on the fact that Barry Buetell would be picked up by the police and placed under arrest for dealing in drugs. I never figured that they had been watching him these past weeks, that they had had him under surveillance and were waiting.

Waiting for him to turn eighteen.

Barry Buetell had the misfortune to turn eighteen on the twenty-eighth of October. By the first of November, the police and detectives followed him to my island and arrested him.

By Monday morning, the whole school knew and everyone, all the faculty and student body, were shocked. Josh and I were not.

By Monday afternoon when I got home, the police car was outside my house. My dad was home. Practically in the middle of the day. And he called me directly into the living room where the two policemen were seated.

I can say in all honesty and without much hesitation that right then and there I was very shocked.

"Brie, did you know anything about drugs buried on your island?" My father had introduced me to the two policemen, Sergeant Bellows and Detective Plebanski. Considering the white look on my father's face, I think he performed the introductions with utmost decorum. He is always a gentleman, my father.

"No, Daddy, I didn't." I managed to say it with a perfectly straight face. Funny, but lying didn't even bother me anymore. What was I supposed to say? I might have been a liar, but I wasn't a crazy person.

"Buetell didn't tell you, when he asked permission to use the island, what he was going to use it for?" asked Sergeant Bellows.

"Fishing," I said innocently. "He said fishing."

"You want to tell me, miss," the detective asked, "what he said to you when he asked you for the use of your island?"

I frowned as if I was trying to remember. That had been weeks ago. After all, how could I be expected

to remember the exact words? I took my time remembering. I lied my head off. The trouble was, I
decided, sitting there while they took notes, I was so
accustomed to lying that I didn't know the truth anymore. And, like all liars, the only thing I could hope
for was that I would keep my lies straight.

They believed me. They listened to my story
about how Buetell had asked me if he could use the
island for fishing. They took notes, they nodded their
heads, they thanked my father, and he saw them out
the door. I didn't bother getting out of my chair, although I could have made a pretty decent escape. I
just sat there. When my dad came back into the
room, he didn't say anything right away. He made a
thorough inspection of his pipe, which seemed to be
giving him all kinds of trouble. He stood in front of
the fireplace fussing with it.

"This wouldn't have anything to do with why you
were there on the island that day with Josh, would it,
Brieanna?"

I felt an enormous sense of relief, even as my mind
worked with ideas converging about what I would
say to him. "Yes, Daddy, it would."

He grunted and sat down. "You want to tell me
about it now?"

And so I told him the only version I could, speaking hesitantly, picking through my choice of words as
I would pick my way through a bed of hot coals,
avoiding the ones that would incriminate me or

render useless all my past lies. I told him someone —and we didn't know who that someone was—had thrust drugs into Josh's hands the night of the party. I told him how I'd taken the drugs and hidden them. And how we went to the island the next day and found them again.

"And what did you do with them then?" he asked.

"We ditched them in the water, Daddy."

He grunted again.

"We didn't know who they belonged to," I added.

He puffed on the pipe thoughtfully. "Why didn't you tell me about it? Why did you put yourself and me through such grief?"

I looked at my hands in my lap. "I was in so much trouble with you, Daddy, for drinking. You were so angry. And you were so down on Josh. I didn't know what to do. I didn't know if you'd believe me if I told you Josh had nothing to do with the drugs. And we didn't want to get the whole class into trouble. We figured those drugs would never be heard from again. If I had *known* it was Buetell who shoved the drugs into Josh's hands, I certainly would never have asked you to let him use the island. I didn't know he had any more drugs there."

"I certainly hope not, Brie. I had some pretty scary moments when I got the call from the police at my office this morning. But they said, right from the beginning, that this Buetell boy told them no one else knew he had drugs there. Still, they had to question you. I'm sorry you had to go through that, honey."

"It's all right, Daddy. Can I be excused?"

"No, I'm not finished. Now that I know the truth about why you went to the island that day, I ought to lift this house arrest I've had you under, shouldn't I?"

I felt a lightness, a surging of joy. "You mean I can go out again? I can go back to the way things were before?"

"You can go out again. Whether either of us can go back to the way things were before is another question."

What did he mean? Was it possible he sensed I was lying? I stole a look at him, but there was no malice in his face, just sadness. "This has been a difficult time for both of us, Brieanna," he said softly. "I feel bad that you didn't come to me with the truth. That you didn't feel comfortable doing that. It makes me examine my performance as a father."

"You just did what you had to do, Daddy," I said generously.

He nodded, still lost in his own thoughts.

"Do you think," I asked cautiously, "that now that you know Josh isn't to blame I could see him again?"

"Ah yes, Josh. I guess I have been rather harsh in judging that boy. Yes, you can see him again. But not every night. I won't have that at your age. You may go out with him but not on school nights. Providing you ask me first and obey all the rules I've set down about dating."

He'd never set down any rules about dating, simply because I'd never really dated much before I met

Josh. Mostly Gina and I had gone out in groups. But
I didn't contest that. I got up and went to him and
leaned over to kiss the side of his face. He was sitting on the couch, and he pulled me down next to
him, with his arm around me, briefly. He hardly ever
did that anymore, hugged me like that. He pressed
me close to him for an instant and kissed the top of
my head. "You're still my little girl, aren't you,
Brieanna?" he asked huskily.

"Yes, Daddy, of course."

"Don't grow up too fast," he said. "You're the last
one I've got. Remember that."

"I will, Daddy." He released me and I moved
away. That evening, right after I phoned Josh to tell
him we could date legitimately, Buetell called.

"Hello, Brie."

I couldn't place his voice for a minute. It was out
of context. I'd never spoken to him on the phone before, and now he was the last person I thought would
ever be calling me. "Well," I said breathlessly,
"hello."

"How you doin'? You sound surprised."

"Well, sure I am. How are you?"

"I'm free on bail. My parents got a good lawyer.
I'm out of school, you know. Randolph doesn't want
me corrupting anybody."

"Barry, I'm sorry," I said. He'd been a good student, and I was sorry to see his school life go down

the drain. "Why did you do it?" I asked. "You, an honor student and everything."

He laughed bitterly. "Why do you think I'm an honor student? Pressure. That's what makes honor students, isn't it? I just couldn't take any more pressure. Does your old man put pressure on you?"

"No. Not to be an honor student. He knows I'll never be one."

"Yeah, well that's just it. He doesn't try to make you something you're not. He accepts you for what you are. You're lucky."

I had never thought about it that way, nor had I thought that Buetell ever looked pressured or anything but cool and indestructible. "I'm really sorry you got kicked out of school, Barry," I said.

"Well, don't be. I don't worry about school. I'm glad the pressure's off. I worry about real things now. Like what they can do to me."

"What can they do to you?"

"The police waited until I was eighteen to nail me as an adult. They've been trailing me for weeks."

He wanted to talk, obviously, so I listened. I was getting the feeling, more and more, as we made small talk that he was leading up to something, that there would be a punch line.

"I gotta promise to do all kinds of handstands now, so I won't be sent off to prison," he said. "It's a first offense. I've got that in my favor."

"You mean plea bargain?" I knew about such

things, because I'd heard my dad talk about it.

"Yeah, I gotta spill my guts. Talk."

"Will you?"

"I'll do anything I can to save my skin."

I felt a cold sweat breaking out all over me. "What are you telling me, Barry?" I whispered urgently into the receiver. "Are you going to say anything about me?"

"Oh, easy, McQuade. I didn't call to upset you. I'm talking about the pushers. Hey, I may be rotten, but I'm not that rotten. You're safe. You did me a favor. Hey, I won't forget it."

"I wish you would, Barry," I said.

He laughed. "Okay then, I will forget it if that's what you want. You have my word. I just called to say thank you for never giving me away. And for everything else."

I felt a flood of sadness. "I'm the one who should be thanking you, Barry. You could have made things awful for me."

"What good would it have done me?"

"None. But you could have anyway. I mean you could have panicked when they picked you up and thought I turned you in."

He laughed. "I know you didn't, McQuade. You had as much to lose as I did. Listen, Brie, I like you. You're a good kid. So I'm gonna tell you something. I may be the only person you know right now who's being really honest with you. That's all I can say.

Except that people aren't always what they seem. Okay?"

Okay? What was he telling me? I stared at the receiver in my darkened room while my nerve endings went raw and my brain went fuzzy. "What do you mean?"

"Just look around you. And be smart. And don't let anybody bust your heart. Okay? You're a nice girl, and I'm sorry for all the hassle I gave you. Good-bye now, Brie. Be smart."

"Barry?"

There was a click. He'd hung up. I sat in the dark in my room, my head reeling with his words, staring at the bright red numbers on my digital clock on my night table. His tone, so urgent, stayed with me. What had he been trying to say? I went to bed, fogged in with my own confusion, and dreamed distorted dreams that made no sense but had an underlying sensation of fear. And in the morning when I woke up, I was exhausted. And that's how I came to the breakfast table when my father told me he was going to get married.

Chapter 16

He was *what?*

"Married, Brie." He smiled at me over his coffee. "You look surprised."

I was not surprised. I was speechless. My mouth was open, forming the disbelief I couldn't put into words.

"It'll probably be right after Christmas," he was saying. "Amanda was talking about the Saturday between Christmas and New Year's. It'll be a small, quiet wedding. Don't tell Alma I said that. She's already got a guest list drawn up. I just want a home reception here."

Reception? The words weren't registering in my mind. He was getting married! Within less than two months! He was sitting there casually telling me about it as if we'd discussed it a dozen times already.

"Why, Daddy?" It was an ungracious question to

ask, I knew that even as I uttered it. But I could think of no words that fit the situation more.

"Why?" The corners of his mouth turned down in that droll smile of his. "We've been going together for a few years now, Brie. Don't you think it's time I made an honest woman of her?"

I nodded as if that was all it took to impose sense on the situation. "You always said..." My voice cracked and I had to start again. "You always said you wouldn't get married until I went away to college."

"That's true, Brie." His voice was very soft and the tone of it was caressing, the way he spoke when he really wanted to charm somebody. "But now I've decided it's unwise to wait. I've decided that I ought to provide you with a more stable home environment. The way things are now, I'm running out of here half the time. You're here with Alma. Or alone. In view of recent events, Brie, I've taken a good hard look at myself and realized that your home atmosphere could be better."

"I'm not complaining, Daddy."

"I know you aren't. I am. I've been pretty harsh with you lately, but I've examined my conscience, as your brother would advise, and decided that your home life isn't all it should be. That I might have been at fault for some of the...lapses of good behavior you've had lately."

I smiled at him weakly. "Daddy, I don't want you getting married on account of me."

"I want to get married, Brie. So does Amanda. I

didn't have to ask her twice. She's been ready for a long time. She's been extremely patient with me, as a matter of fact." He scowled. "You're not going to oppose this, are you?"

I shook my head, no.

"You and Amanda seem to be getting along fine. I know you've had your difficulties in the past, but I was under the impression that you've ironed them all out."

"We have, Daddy. I'm just a little surprised, that's all."

"Well, I'm sorry about that. It was a sudden decision. We talked and decided we're both ready. I'm tired of running out of here every Saturday night like a teenager on a date. And so is she. Now"—he smiled at me—"I think it would be nice if you wished Amanda well the first chance you get, don't you?"

"Yes, Daddy." My mind was settling down. It wasn't the worst thing in the world, after all, and my old dad did deserve to be happy. I sort of pulled myself together from some reserve of strength I didn't know I had, and something told me that he was waiting to be congratulated. Or at least that it was the right thing to do. I wasn't entirely self-centered, after all. So I got up and went to him and put my arms around him and kissed his cheek. "Congratulations, Daddy," I murmured.

There was a catch in my voice. Because I really meant it, I discovered. "Thanks, sweetie," he said.

"Now I want you to sit down and listen to me again because there's more I have to tell you. And the next thing isn't so pleasant."

More? How could there be more? I couldn't take any more. But I sat down, waiting.

"Brieanna," he said quietly, and I knew it was serious because he called me Brieanna instead of Brie. "Your brother is talking about leaving the priesthood."

I felt the earth shake beneath me as I met his eyes across the table. I saw him watching my face for its expression. I said nothing.

"Did you know about this?" he asked.

I clasped and unclasped my hands in my lap. "I..." My voice wasn't working again. I ran my tongue along my lips and started once more. "He said something to me just once. A while back. But I thought he was joking."

"He isn't joking. He's perfectly serious. Of course, I don't know why." He looked into his coffee cup as if something unusual in the brew demanded close scrutiny. "He hasn't told me why. Apparently I'm not to be the beneficiary of that information. Do you have any idea what's going on with him?"

"No, Daddy." Idea? I had a darned good idea. But I wasn't going to rat on Kev anymore than he would rat on me.

"And you wouldn't tell me if you did know, right?"

I shrugged.

"Look, I know you and Kev keep secrets from me.

It's okay. But I also know you two have a system of checks and balances on each other. I depend on each of you to keep the other honest. Listen, Brie, I've seen something coming for a long time now with Kevin. I don't know what brought it on. But the signs have been there. The problem with Manuel, for instance, was indicative of something. You yourself saw that. You thought I was unconcerned when you brought it up with me. I guess I appear kind of unconcerned about my kids sometimes. But I'm not."

He paused for a moment, looked to see what effect this was having on me and went on. "I've been watching both you and Kev this fall. Watching you evolve and make your mistakes. Oh, I've been on you, sure. But allowing you to go out with Josh was one instance when I just sat back and held my breath and waited. And hoped you'd handle it right. And I've been watching Kev muck his way through his problems. It isn't easy to sit back, Brie, and allow your kids enough room to make their own mistakes. You don't know how much it hurts to keep your hands off as a parent. A good parent does that, tries to walk the line between letting the kids go and keeping them from hurting themselves. Or others. It's been hard for me to keep my hands off when I know both you and Kev needed a lot of help this fall. I do a lot of praying, Brie. Sometimes more than Kev."

The room was very silent. I didn't say anything. There isn't anything you can say when your father says something like that to you. I just waited.

He went on. "It ties in with what I told you before about commitment after disillusionment. Kev has to go through his disillusionment before he realizes he's really committed to the priesthood. I've seen some of the pitfalls he has, and I've shut up about them. I'm not saying I know all Kev's problems. I sense there's more than he's telling me these days. I do know, however, that one of the girls in the home had an abortion a few days ago. She apparently never wanted the baby and was there at the urging of some do-good social worker. Kev was working with her. Trying, anyway. I think that had a lot to do with his decision. He let something slip to me that he's a failure as a priest."

"He's a good priest, Daddy," I said vehemently.

"I know that, Brie. So do you and so do a lot of people. Apparently Kev doesn't. Yet. *But he has to find it out for himself.* It isn't anything I can give him."

My coffee was cold. But I drank it. It left a stale taste in my mouth.

"There're times when parents just have to back off," he said. "However, we have our emissaries." He smiled. "You know how to get around your brother. I'd like you to go over there and see him this morning. Just check in with him and make sure he's all right. Will you do that for me?"

"Sure, Daddy. I'm going to the football game this afternoon with Josh, but I've got the whole morning."

"Thank you, Brie," he said. And then he started

reading his newspaper. I kissed him again before I left. He smiled vaguely and patted my arm. It seems as if whenever I start to see my father for the wonderful person he really is, just when he starts to reveal himself to me, he backs off and retreats again. I left him there reading his paper.

I never went to St. Hedwig's rectory if I could help it. I didn't like it. It's an old house with high ceilings, and floors that creak, and lots of dark woodwork. The only room I feel good in is Kev's office, but even there the walls are a colorless plaster. Kev has this big old desk with papers piled all over it. They aren't his, he says. They belong to Father Roland. He doesn't want to disturb anything or put anything to rights, because that would almost indicate that he intended to make himself at home at St. Hedwig's. And Kev never lets himself forget that he's only there temporarily. The office has a nice Oriental rug on the floor, which is a warm touch. In a far corner, Father Roland has some boxes of papers. Kev doesn't live like that. He doesn't like clutter. He lives sparingly, which is why he prefers to use the office at Second Chance.

He has a housekeeper at the parish house. Felicity is her name. She's a real mother figure, and he says he hates her fussing about him. But secretly I think he enjoys the attention. Part of Kev's trouble is that his mother walked off when he was seventeen.

Felicity was out when I rang the front door bell. So

Kev answered it. He smiled wanly, shrugged, and bade me follow him inside. He had interrupted a phone conversation with a parishioner whose mother had just died. He'd been there with the dying woman the night before, he told me. I sat down in a chair and waited, pretending not to be interested. But I watched him as he counseled the woman on the phone. He did a lot of listening, of course, and when he spoke, it was in soothing, reassuring tones. Then he put down the phone and grinned at me.

"Hi, Kev."

"How you doing? You're on parole, I hear. And Dad's allowing you to go out with Josh again."

"Yeah. We're going to a football game this afternoon."

He looked more tired than ever, and the ashtray on the desk was filled with cigarette butts. But he gave me the old Irish grin. "You amaze me, Brieanna. You come out standing on your feet all the time. Not only that, Dad's been telling me how he thinks he misjudged Josh. He actually feels bad about it, do you know that?"

"Is it true that you're leaving the priesthood, Kev?"

He didn't react. His blue, level gaze just stayed locked into mine. "Who's the inquisitor in this outfit, anyway?"

"Are you?" I demanded. I wasn't going to let him charm me now, I knew that much. Like Dad, he knew when to lay the charm on.

"The thought has crossed my mind."

"You told Dad."

"Ah, so that's it. Dad sent you here."

"How many times has he sent you to work on me?"

His smile deepened. "We got ourselves some old man, you know that, Brieanna? He worries himself like a housemother over both of us."

"You can't leave the priesthood, Kev. You just can't."

"Well, I admit it isn't that easy a thing to pull off. They don't go out of their way to make it easy."

"That's not what I mean. You know what I mean."

His smile vanished. "I'll be fine, Brieanna," he said sadly. "Don't worry about me."

"Sure, maybe you'll be fine, although I doubt it. But what'll it do to Dad?"

"Hey, he never wanted me to be a priest in the first place."

"He never tried to stop you, Kev. And I just wish you could know what your being a priest means to him. I can't even joke about it in front of him. He gets spastic if I do."

For once in his life, he didn't throw me a wise remark. "I'm not a very good priest, Brieanna. That's the bottom line of it."

"That's garbage. Some stupid girl runs off and gets an abortion. She was probably planning on doing it all along. You're not responsible for everybody."

"Thank you, Brieanna. I appreciate what you're trying to do. But it so happens that I was somewhere else the day that girl needed me."

"So? Do you have to hold their hands? Isn't it enough that you started the home for them? That you gave the house our grandmother left you to their cause and fought everybody in town to get the zoning changed so the house could open? And besides that, you're running this whole parish and you know how you hate parish work. It isn't your thing. You're tired, Kev, that's what's wrong with you."

"People are my thing." He said it so calmly it maddened me. "I only know that. I wasn't here for that girl when she needed me. I was somewhere else. Somewhere I wasn't supposed to be. And I wasn't here for Manuel when he needed me, either."

"Are we back on Manuel again?"

"I never left the subject of Manuel. And where was I the day you needed me? When you wanted to talk. You ended up going to the island with Josh."

"I just wish everybody would forget that day," I said miserably.

"I pushed you aside for my own reasons that day. I seem to have a knack for doing that with people."

"Kev, all I know is that you're a good priest."

"Was." He smiled wanly at me. "I *was* a good priest. But it all seems to be coming apart. I couldn't help you. These past few months, you were in a lot of pain and confusion, and I couldn't get through to you. How do you think I feel about that?"

"You helped me, Kev. Lots."

"These past couple of months"—he went on as if I hadn't even spoken—"look what you've been going

through. Dad told me what happened when you
went to the island that day with Josh. I don't know
why you couldn't have told me that you had to go
back to the island and get rid of the drugs."

I thought my heart would stop beating there for a
minute. If he knew the real story! He'd feel worse!
"I almost told you a couple of times. Once I had to
run out of Second Chance because I wanted to tell
you so bad, honest."

"Well, it's my job not only to help the poor and
open houses for unwed mothers, but to be there for
people like you who are right in front of my nose
screaming for help. I've missed those people. Right
down the line. I've concentrated so much on the
poor that I couldn't see the problems of the middle
class for looking. I tell you honestly, Brie, I don't
want to see the problems of the middle class. Oh, I'm
not talking about you. I'm talking about these people
in this parish. Their problems are endless, and I find
myself getting annoyed. They've got everything material in the world. I'm used to dealing with the poor
who have nothing. I just can't get up any compassion
for these people. And I know that's wrong."

We were both quiet. What could I say to that? I
struggled for the right words, but I could see I was
losing. He was so good with words himself. It was as
if words, coming from someone else, just bounced off
him. Like he'd been through them all so often before
that they were worn out and used up by now.

I couldn't help him. I wasn't up to it. "Does Diana

have anything to do with this?" I asked.

He sighed. "She's part of it. But she's not the real reason. Diana wouldn't be any more than a leaf in the wind if I wasn't shaken in my beliefs to begin with. She's just there. She's not the cause. She's just there."

"She always did know the right time to be there, too, Kev."

He got up. The discussion was over. "I'm going to ignore that. I'm not doing anything rash, Brieanna, I promise. You can tell Dad that. I have a lot of agonizing to do first. I'm not about to rip off my cassock and don a pin-striped suit. Now go along to your football game and don't worry about me. I mean it."

He walked me to the front door. "Don't worry," he insisted. "This isn't something a person rushes into. They don't let you do it that way."

"Do they let you do it at all?"

"Not in any way a person can live with, no. But if I did it, I'd learn to live with it. I promise."

"Isn't there anything that could change your mind and make you feel good about yourself again?"

He thought for a moment. "If I could go back and do right some of the things I've done wrong lately. If I could make amends with just one person. But we don't get the chance to do that in life, do we? Could I change what happened the day you went to the island? It's too late to help you with that anymore." He closed his eyes and shook his head.

I felt the blood rush from my head. I got white in

the face. Then it all seemed to rush back again until I was hot and flushed. I turned away so he wouldn't see.

"Incidentally, when are you coming back to church?" he asked. "I'm not finished with you yet. I'm still planning on conducting the Inquisition. I've got the rack and thumbscrews all ready in the basement."

"Kevin McQuade"—I looked him straight in the eye—"I'll never step foot inside a church again if you leave the priesthood."

He drew me to him and kissed my forehead. "That doesn't work with me and you know it. I taught you a long time ago that everyone is responsible for their own salvation. Go on now. Enjoy your football game. We'll talk again soon."

He was smiling at me in the doorway of St. Hedwig's parish house when I left. I took his smile with me into the bright November day. I knew what I was going to do before I was down the steps of the front stoop, of course. I knew it as soon as he'd told me what it would take to make him change his mind.

It was so simple. I was one of the ones he had failed. Just one person, he'd said. If he could make it up to just one person.

Chapter 17

What would he do if he left the priesthood? String beads? Paint signs? Sell insurance? It was crazy! It made no sense. He was so much a priest, he could never stop being one. He couldn't even go into the newspaper business with Dad. He wasn't cut out for that.

I had to stop him from doing it.

My father was out when I got home. I was just as glad. I needed time alone, time to think. Leave the priesthood! A priest was all I had known Kevin to be and all that he planned on being since I was a little girl. His priesthood was part of my identity. My brother the priest. Sure, I got annoyed at the remarks sometimes, but there was always a warm, good feeling inside me whenever I thought of Kev and what he was doing. Our family was pretty messed up otherwise, when you really think about it, what with my mom leaving when I was two and Dad being alone all those years. And then Dad going with Amanda for so long without any plans for marriage. Through it all, Kev was the one who always had a handle on things, the one who was the ballast, the one who kept everything together.

Boy, I was annoyed with Kev now! Why should I have to worry about something like this on such a beautiful day? And it had turned out beautiful. The sun had warmed nicely, everything was blue and gold. The leaves were almost all down, and the sun filtered through the costume colors of the ones that remained on the trees. There was a special kick in the air. Why couldn't I just forget about Kev and enjoy the day and the game and my date with Josh like any other normal sixteen-year-old? Because of my stupid family, that's why. I wasn't the kid in the family, not really. They wouldn't let me be, either Dad or Kev. And I resented it, even as I loved them at the moment. Bitterly.

I must have been awfully quiet in the car on the way to the game. "Glad to see you so happy and sociable," Josh said.

I smiled. "I'm sorry. I was just thinking."

"Yeah, I know. The air is filled with pollution."

He looked great in his jeans and tweed jacket and crewneck sweater. He looked like an ad for a man's cologne or one of those designer menswear ads in which everybody is standing around watching polo games. Nobody could wear jeans and look like an

heir apparent like Josh could.

"Where you wanna go after the game?" he asked.

"Doesn't this time of year make you sad, Josh?"

"No. I like it. I love the weather. Are you sad?"

"Not sad, really. I just sort of feel the weight of the whole year on me." It was a dumb adolescent remark, but he didn't laugh.

"I know what you mean," he said. "This time of year can do that to you if you let it. Look, how 'bout we take a nice ride out into the country after the game?"

"I wanna go to the refuge, Josh," I said. "I want to see the animals."

Before we even got to the football field, we could hear the distant rumble of drums from the school band. It was the yearly rivalry game—Coreysville against Waltham High. I didn't really care about football, and I knew Josh didn't either, but he was doing a color piece on the old rivalry game for the school paper. And so we sat in the stands and ate the required hot dogs and yelled the required yells when Waltham scored, carried along on the tide of color and noise and excitement. Josh got up and walked around a lot, talking to people and getting quotes for his story. The special effects of the day were great, of course. Waltham High won, and the band and the cheerleaders and fans went crazy. Josh held my hand as he guided me down the bleachers. It took a long time to get out of the place, and then as we came around the corner of the school, I could see the yellow buses that had brought the Coreysville players and saw bunches of them standing around, dirty and disconsolate. And then I saw that some of them were crying. Real tears were coming down their faces as they stood holding their helmets in their hands. I was shocked to see that. Hulking football players, red-eyed, dirt-streaked faces contorted, crying. Over a game. It's only a *game*, I wanted to yell at them. I must have stood staring for a minute, because the next thing I knew Josh was tugging me. "Come on!" he insisted. He didn't say anything, but I knew he saw them crying too.

"What's wrong?" he asked. We were in the parking lot across from school. He was throwing the stadium blankets into the back seat. I got in.

"Nothing."

He got in and slammed the door on his side. "Come on, what is it?"

"Did you see those kids crying?"

"Yeah. I saw them. Idiots."

"Why is it that a game is suddenly not important to me, Josh?" I asked. "Am I abnormal or something?"

"You've got something else on your mind," he said. "I knew that the minute I picked you up today. You wanna tell me what it is?"

"Kev is thinking of leaving the priesthood." It was the first time I'd uttered those words to anybody, and they seemed like treason coming out of my mouth, as if my saying them gave them credibility. "I really need somebody to talk to about it."

"Is this for real or is it something you're imagining, Brie?"

"It's real. He told me this morning."

He gave a low whistle and was silent for a few minutes. I could tell that even he was impressed. "Is it the girl?" he asked.

"I don't know. I thought it was her, and I'm sure she's got something to do with it. But there's lots of other things too. He says he's failed too many people, that he's not a good priest. He admits he doesn't like parish work, and he knows he's wrong for not being able to understand the people around here. I'm gonna have to help him, Josh."

"How?"

I looked at him cautiously. "I wanted to talk to you first. Since it involves both of us. I'm gonna go to him for confession. I'm gonna tell him what really happened with the drugs on the island."

"You want to tell him you were an accomplice in hiding drugs? To make him feel better? Oh great, that oughta go over big with him right now."

"Josh, I asked him if anything would make him feel better about himself as a priest. He said yes. If he could go back and undo some of the failures he's committed with people. Well, he says he failed Manuel. I told you about him. And the girl who left Second Chance to have an abortion. I didn't tell you about that yet. But he says he was somewhere else

when she needed him. I think he was with Diana.
And he says he failed me. The day I ran off with you
to the island."

Josh looked at me. "Did he?"

"Sort of. Yes. If I really want to be honest, I have
to say yes. I ran out to talk to him. I just wanted to
get him away from Diana at first. Then we argued,
and he walked off with her. He acted like he didn't
care if I needed him. I was sore and really sick over
seeing him and her go off together. Then you called.
Dad told me not to go to the island again. He told me
not to see you. But I went. Who knows? If Kev
hadn't run off with Diana—"

"Boy, that's stretching it," Josh said.

"Yeah, well, call it what you want. Kev failed me
that day, and he knows it."

"So why do you have to go to confession? Why not
just talk to him?"

We were driving along the river. Josh had the radio
on low and the sun was still warm coming in the car
window and it was all very pleasant. "Because," I
said, "because I have to let him help me as a priest. I
have to let him make things right again with one person. And because he can't give away any secrets that
way. I'm telling him stuff about a lot of people, Josh.
You and Barry Buetell, for one. It has to be this way,
that's all."

We drove in silence for a while. "Do whatever you
think is best," Josh said finally. "He's your brother."

* * *

The sun was starting to go down by the time the little sports car climbed the hill at the refuge. The place was very quiet, and it was that special time of day between sunset and dusk. We stood on top of the hill after we got out of the car, looking at the last rays of the sun touching the river in the distance. The day was fading into a purple memory that seemed to fall like a mantle over everything. I felt a strange sense of release, even peace.

"Let's go see the animals," I said.

He took my hand and we walked toward the outside compound. Right away, the geese saw us and came over to greet us. I wished I'd brought some bread. Sinbad the crow was jumping around in his huge cage, fastening his beady eyes on us and waiting. I didn't feel so bad about not bringing the bread when Josh said he was going to feed the animals. He was scheduled to do so. And he said I could help him. So we spent almost an hour doing that. Josh made a ritual of it, talking to Madame Pompadour and the opossum and the squirrels and calling all the geese by name. We both avoided Confucius's cage, although when we were finished, Josh stood there looking at it from a distance, not saying anything.

"Where do you think he is?" I asked softly.

He shrugged.

"Do you think he's on his way to South America or someplace?"

"Wherever he feels he has to go, that's where he's on his way to," Josh said.

"Do you think he'll show up around here someday?"

Again he shrugged. I could tell he found it difficult
to talk about the old owl who used to cluck at him in
warning. "I don't know," he said hoarsely. "All I
know is that every time I hear one outside the window at night, I'll sure think it's him."

"Josh, I'm glad we have this place to come to together," I said. "You know what? I like it even better
than my island."

On the way home, it was as if we were trying to
make the day last forever. We stopped at an artsy-
craftsy mini-mall, and I bought my dad some of his
favorite tobacco. I felt good. Being at the refuge with
Josh always made me feel better, as if some order
were being imposed on my own chaotic world. Josh
bought me a hamburger and shake, and on the way
home, I fancied I could smell the wood smoke from
people's houses as we drove into my neighborhood.
Josh pulled the car up in front of the house, and we
sat there for a while saying nothing.

"Can you come in?" I asked.

"No. I gotta go home and write the article on the
game for the paper. Hey, you cold?"

I was, suddenly. My sweater wasn't warm enough,
so Josh reached around to the back seat and handed
me something. "Here, put this on."

"Josh, it's your good sweatshirt." He'd thrust it into
my lap, and I recognized it instantly as his favorite.

The heavy gray one with the blue lettering in front that said Chittendon.

I put it on. "I'll give it back to you tomorrow."

"No. You can keep it."

I stared at him. "But it's your favorite! It means so much to you."

"Nah. I don't wanna wear it anymore."

"Why not?"

"I'm just..." He waved his hand and leaned back with his head against the seat, closing his eyes. "I'm sick of the whole thing. Tired of it. I don't want to be reminded of the place anymore. It's still a good sweatshirt, though. I want you to have it, honest."

Again we both fell silent. The sadness that he was feeling underneath was contagious. I felt the day receding all around me. It was dark, and with the dark came my fears. Everything took on a different perspective. I shuddered, allowing the thoughts I'd fended off all afternoon to creep into my consciousness. They came like goblins on Halloween, in distorted shapes and with leering faces.

My father was getting married. How much difference would that make in my life? What would Amanda be like when she really started living in the house? Sure, we got along now, but would she change things?

And what about children? Amanda was still young enough to have children. How would I feel if she suddenly came up pregnant? They had never promised me they wouldn't have children. Still, wasn't my dad too old to start over again? I knew how I would feel. Disinherited, nothing less.

And then there was Kev leaving the priesthood. I couldn't even speculate what that would mean in my life or to any of us. And next to me sat Josh, whom I loved but who, for some unexplainable reason, never even put his arms around me and kissed me. Josh, who would never be happy, who had left part of his soul back at that stupid military school in Pennsylvania. And what had I vowed to do, so coolly, a few hours ago? Go to Kev for confession? Was I crazy?

The wind was picking up, kicking dead leaves around, casting shadows that made me see things lurking behind trees. I could feel my spirits falling, feel one of my blackest moods taking over. The whole world looked wrong and frightening. Josh leaned toward me, picking up on my mood. He touched my hair. I shivered. His closeness did that to me. I raised my eyes to him appealingly. I could smell the fragrance of his after-shave. That's what did me in, I think, what pushed me over the edge.

"You've been great, Josh. I don't know what I'd do without you."

"Yeah, well, you're okay yourself."

"Hold me," I said.

He smiled.

"Please." I knew I was begging, but I didn't care. He put his arm around me. "Come on, now, you're taking the whole world on your shoulders. If your brother wants to leave the priesthood, it isn't your fault. You can't stop him."

"Kiss me, Josh."

"Hey, come on, what's wrong?"

"I want you to kiss me. Does something have to be wrong?"

"You know what I told you about me and girls. People get hurt when you get involved. I don't wanna hurt you."

"I'm not gonna get hurt if you kiss me."

He kissed my forehead.

"Josh!" I pulled back, indignantly. "That's how Kev kisses me!"

"Look, Brie—"

"No, you look. You know how long we've been going together? Why do you go out with me? We don't have to get involved. Not like you did at Chittendon. Isn't there any other way for you?"

He sighed. "Don't do this, Brie."

"Do what? What am I doing?"

"Don't push it."

"Push it? Okay, maybe I am pushing it. But you know what I think? I don't believe this stuff about you never wanting to get close to another girl. I think there's something wrong with me."

"There's nothing wrong with you, Brie."

"Well, what am I supposed to think? That's all I've been thinking lately." I started to cry. "There must be something wrong with me. I think the only reason

you go out with me is because I like to go up to the
refuge with you and I don't laugh at it. But you sure
don't like me because of me, I can tell you that."

"Hey, cut that out!" He was angry. "What do you
mean I don't like you because of you? That's a hell of
a thing to say."

I sniffled for a few minutes. He gave me a handkerchief. "You know better than that, Brie," he said
gently. His voice brushed against me tenderly.
"Come on, huh?" he coaxed.

I didn't answer.

"What's wrong isn't with you, Brie. You hear me?
You understand?"

"I hear you, but I don't understand."

He sighed. "I like you, Brie. I love you, really. As
a friend. As a sister."

"A sister! What does that mean?"

"We're friends."

"What are you telling me?"

"Don't do this to yourself. Or to me. That's what
I'm telling you. It's been so beautiful, our friendship. Like tonight. Wasn't tonight beautiful? Going
to the refuge? Talking and sharing things? Don't
ruin it, Brie. Don't make me ruin it for you."

Buetell's words came to my mind then for some
crazy reason. "Don't let anybody bust your heart. I
may be the only person you know right now who's
being really honest with you." I felt a tremor of fear
short-circuit my senses.

"I don't understand, Josh. What are you trying to

tell me? What could you ruin for me?"

"Everything." In the dark, I made out his grin, then it faded.

"What am I doing to ruin things? Josh?"

"Nothing, Brie. You're doing nothing wrong. This just isn't the time, that's all, with everything else you've been through today."

"The time for what?"

"To tell you."

"Tell me"—I could barely form the words—"what?"

He shook his head. "You're really gonna push it, aren't you? You're not gonna let it go."

"No, Josh. You have something to tell me, you'd better tell me. Or I'm not leaving this car. I'm not getting out."

"I planned on telling you, Brie. Sooner or later. I hoped it could be later. I was hoping—"

"Tell me what?"

I'd always known there was something about him, of course, that made it impossible for him to love me. But then why did the whole world move under me when he said it?

"You know Colonel Sequist's daughter? Back at Chittendon?"

"Yes."

"Well, he didn't have a daughter. He had a son. I'm a homosexual, Brie. I'm sorry."

Chapter 18

When I awoke the next morning, I was surprised to find that I'd slept in my clothes, on top of the bed covers. I was still wearing the gray sweatshirt. I sat up, cleared my head, and looked down at it.

On my chest were emblazoned the blue letters. Chittendon. Talk about your scarlet letter! I pulled off the sweatshirt and stumbled around my room aimlessly for a few minutes. It was raining outside, a fine sleeting-type November rain. The temperature had dropped overnight, and I shivered, seeing the cold rain slash against the windows. A hot shower, that's what I needed. I made it down the hall to the bathroom, stripped off my clothes as if I wanted nothing more to do with anything that reminded me of last night, and got under the shower.

Last night! I shuddered as the fragmented parts of

the memory fell together. I know I cried last night. My sore eyes and head attested to that. I remember grabbing his jacket and asking him *what did he mean!* Stupid. He'd said it plain enough. But he said it again for me, patiently.

I think it was then that I hit him. I don't know if it was once or a lot of times, but I remember grabbing his sweater in front. I know I called him awful names. I know I yelled until my voice got hoarse, and he covered my mouth with his hand and told me they'd hear me. My father and Amanda were home, inside the house. I calmed myself then, managed somehow to stop my sobs, and somehow got myself in the house through the back door and up the stairs before anybody saw me. I figured I looked awful.

I remembered all of that. But what I remembered most of all were the words he'd said to to me. I know that as long as I lived I would never forget their terrifying simplicity.

"You know Colonel Sequist's daughter? Well, he didn't have a daughter. He had a son."

Words don't do it in the end, I've decided. They're stupid, shallow. They don't cover the awfulness of things that sometimes have to be said. Or sometimes have to be listened to. They certainly don't add up to the horror they sometimes cause. And in the end, they just lay there between two people like empty symbols that have done their horrible work, that have ruined everything.

* * *

I got dressed somehow and took my aching head down to breakfast. My father was having one of his distracted mornings, thank heaven, one of his read-the-Sunday-paper-and-make-abstract-conversation mornings. He inquired politely how I was, and I answered, politely, that I was just fine, thank you. A little tired. He commented about Waltham's win over Coreysville the day before. A thousand years before, to me. And I mumbled something about it being great. I reached for coffee, told him I had a headache, and he told me to get some aspirin from the kitchen.

"We've missed mass again, both of us," he said. "Kev'll be on me again. I really think you ought to start thinking about going to church on Saturday nights, Brie."

He seemed to have forgotten that his son was talking about leaving the priesthood. Or was it so automatic with him to think of Kev as a priest that he could never do otherwise? Oh, I couldn't cope with it all. My head was pounding. I ate some breakfast so he wouldn't suspect any trouble with me. And then I asked to be excused. I had some studying to do, I said. He said all right. He said Amanda was coming for Sunday dinner and I should try to get rid of my headache before then.

I took some books into the living room with a cup of coffee and put on the lamps and wrapped myself in an afghan and pretended to study. I leaned my head

against the side of the wing chair and closed my
eyes. The house was silent. Alma was at church. My
father was still in the dining room. Inside my eyelids, I could see Josh's face, the familiar contour of his
head, with the hair just always a little shorter than the
other guys at school in deference to his military background. I stared into my coffee cup, remembering
how he'd looked when he'd released Confucius, arms
upraised as if he was part of the great bird. And then
I felt an overwhelming sense of grief that seemed to
well up from places inside me that I didn't even
know I had. And the tears started coming down my
face. I heard a car pull into the driveway, heard my
father go to the hall and greet someone at the door. I
wiped my tears hastily, but they both went back to
the dining room. I heard my father offer whoever it
was coffee. Somehow I will get through today, I told
myself.

So this was why Gina had not wanted me to go out
with him. Sitting there, I remembered her then. "If
you have an ounce of brains in your head, you'll stay
away from him, Brie. I don't know how else to tell
you." So this was what Buetell meant when he'd
said, "Don't let anybody break your heart." Somehow Buetell must have suspected.

The Joshua Falcone I had loved did not exist. He
had never existed. I had invented him, because I
needed someone like him in my life. The boy who
had filled the part had done so like an actor assuming
a role in a movie. And now the movie was over, and

it was time to emerge into the reality of everyday light.

I told no one. Josh had asked me not to, and I knew I would honor that request. He had also told me he was celibate, that he had been ever since he'd left Chittendon. "You know, like your brother, Kev." There was AIDS to consider, he'd said. It was all very much in the headlines. He had not been with anyone since the business at Chittendon, he'd told me. I didn't want to think of what he'd meant by that. All I knew was that my beautiful Josh with the charming smile, the beautiful shoulders, the military bearing, was not what he'd passed himself off as being.

I tried to integrate the fact of his homosexuality into my life. I made an honest effort to fit it in, but it wouldn't integrate. The terrible fact of it had to be absorbed into everything I did and felt and considered. I found that difficult. Josh was right there in my thoughts all the time. He had been for months. But whenever I thought of him, I'd have to stop and say no, I can't do this, I can't think of him that way anymore. He's a homosexual!

I found myself stumbling through the next few days making my moves automatically. What I was not prepared for was seeing him again. I did not want to see him again. How would I act with him? I was terrified of confronting him, as a matter of fact. What was I to say? Nothing in my life had prepared me for all of this. So, the first time I did see him in school, I broke into tears and ran the other way.

He followed me. He caught up with me in the library. I should have fled to the girls' room, I realized too late. He found me in the biography section in front of Abraham Lincoln.

"Hello, Brie."

How could he? How could he just walk up and say hello like that? You don't do that after an earthquake. I clutched a biography of Abraham Lincoln to my breast and stared at him.

"Are you all right?" he asked.

I know what I looked like, wild-eyed and breathless from running. I know there wasn't any blood left in my face. "I'm fine."

"Hey, come on, I'm still Josh. The same guy you've always known. I'm not gonna bite you."

"What do you want?"

"I want to know if you're okay. You've been avoiding me."

Was he crazy? What did he expect me to do? "I don't know what you want from me," I said. "I just wish you'd leave me alone."

"You look awful."

"Thank you."

"Have you been sleeping at all? Hasn't your father asked any questions? Your eyes are purple underneath."

"My father left Monday afternoon for an editors' convention in Washington." It was true. He'd be away all week, conveniently. All I had was Alma, and she could be gotten around and lied to. Kev would come over once in a while and check on things, but he had so much trouble of his own that he wouldn't notice how I looked. I hoped.

"Brie, I'm sorry."

Sorry? I couldn't believe he was saying those words. How could such words cover it? "Sorry for what?"

"For what I did to you."

"What you did to me . . . ?" My voice trailed off, and I tried to focus my thoughts. I looked at his face, the face I'd known so well, where I'd found friendship and trust, and it was like an old road map that didn't work anymore. Because someone had come through town and torn down all the old places and put up a parking lot.

"Why did you date me?" I asked. "Was it just a cover-up?"

"No. Honest, Brie. I really like you as a friend." He shrugged. "Any other girls I might have dated since I came back to Waltham were cover-ups, though. For looks. To keep my family happy."

"Do you know how . . . I felt about you?"

"That's what I'm sorry for, Brie. I never realized it was going this far."

"What did you think I was doing? Seeing you for my health? Climbing out of windows and getting into trouble with my dad, maybe, because of you? What did you think . . . ?" I couldn't go on.

"Oh, geez, Brie, don't cry."

"Would you let me by, please? I think I want to leave here now."

He wasn't really blocking my way, and he would have moved in a minute. What I wanted was for him to let me go, to be done with me. "I wanna talk. Let me drive you home."

"No."

"Let's go for a ride to the refuge. Let's go see the animals."

"No."

"Don't you miss Sinbad? We'll feed the geese."

"Stop it!"

"I can't stand seeing you like this. How are you making it in class?"

"Don't worry about me. I'm fine."

"Brie, I haven't changed. I care about you. Please, let's take a ride up to the refuge. We'll talk."

I thought my heart would burst. "How can you even say that?"

"I'm saying it and meaning it. You're a friend. That's what I always hoped we could be. That's why I never wanted sex to get in the way. We had a beautiful friendship, didn't we?"

"You did."

"We both did. We don't have to let it go. We can still have it. Don't you see? Because of what I am, we can be friends forever. *Forever*, Brie. Even after you're grown-up and married. How many guys can you say that about? Isn't that worth holding on to?"

I stared at him. Grown-up and married? I just

wanted to get through this afternoon. This next hour!

"Will you come for a ride with me and let me explain some things to you?"

"No."

"Then talk to somebody, please. Let somebody else explain things to you."

What was he saying? I tried to focus my thoughts, but I couldn't keep my eyes from him. It was a shock to see that he was the same, physically, as he'd always been. That he hadn't changed overnight.

"I'm worried about you, Brie. And I feel responsible. I think you should talk to somebody else if you won't talk to me."

"Somebody else? Who?"

He gave that little downward curve of a smile of his. "Did you do what you said you were going to do? With Kev?"

"Of course not." Go to confession to Kev? It was out of the question now. Ridiculous. The idea had always been ridiculous. Certainly, I could never go to Kev now. I shrank from the very idea of opening my heart and my soul to anybody.

"Why not?" he persisted.

"I don't need any help."

"You can't keep it bottled up inside you."

"Kev has enough on his mind."

"Are you sure that's it? Or are you just being selfish?"

"You're crazy," I said. "I never knew how crazy you were until now."

"Maybe I am. But I accepted what I am a long time ago, Brie. My mistake was in not telling you sooner. I'm sorry about that, and now I want to help you. Okay, you won't let me. But you should let someone else help you. I don't mind your telling Kevin. He'll keep it quiet and explain things to you. Then maybe you'll talk to me again."

I was about to push past him in the aisle, but I hesitated. Something in his voice, his tone, appealed to me. Something of the old Josh was still there somewhere inside. Could it be possible? I pushed the thought aside, and he stepped away and let me pass. But the tone of his words stayed with me as I walked out into the hall. He didn't follow.

Chapter 19

I managed to elude him for a week. I timed my whereabouts in school so they wouldn't coincide with his. Luckily, I knew his schedule. Once I saw him in the cafeteria. I got out of there quickly. Another time, when I wanted fresh air between classes on a warm November day, I sauntered out onto the smoking patio. I didn't smoke and neither did he. But he found me. I looked up from where I was seated on a low brick wall, and he was just there.

I looked right into those blue eyes of his. "Did you talk to him yet?" he asked.

"Who?"

"You know who."

"Go away."

"I hear you flunked geometry on the midterm."

"What are you, my father or something? I don't need you checking up on me."

"Doesn't your old man ask questions? You look as if you're losing weight."

"I told you he was away. He just got back last night."

"Do me a favor, Brie. Talk to Kev. Haven't you seen him? Hasn't he noticed anything strange about you?"

"I've managed to avoid Kev, thank you."

"I'm not gonna leave you alone until you tell me you at least talked to Kev. I'll follow you all over school. I'll make you miserable."

"You already have."

"Good." He smiled. "I didn't mean that, Brie. I love you. Honest. I know you don't understand that now. Maybe someday you will. Tomorrow I'm gonna ask you again if you saw Kev."

"Good. Meet me here tomorrow. I'll give you back your sweatshirt."

He'd started to walk away, then he turned, straight and tall, framed against the brick of the building. "Keep the sweatshirt. I gave it to you."

"It says Chittendon on it," I said bitterly.

"Yeah, well throw it away then. I don't want it back. I gave it to you. Do what you want with it."

I knew I'd never be able to throw it away. I knew I'd probably keep it forever. I'd find it someday in my things when I was old and married.

"Go see Kev, will you, Brie?"

"No," I said. "For once and for all. No."

"You're really a selfish kid. You know that?"

I stared at him. Tears came to my eyes, because I
saw that he meant it, and because I still cared what
he thought about me. I tried to speak but couldn't.

"You were going to play faith healer awhile back.
You were all ready to go to your brother and save him
from himself. You really thought you could do that.
You were going to make him think you needed him.
And, now . . . ?"

I opened my mouth to speak, but he interrupted.
"Now that you really do need him, you won't go to
him at all. So I call that selfish."

Before I could even form a retort, he turned and
walked away. The bell rang for classes, but I sat
there on the smoking patio and didn't move. So I'd
miss science, so what? The world would go on, just
as crummy as it had been going on for zillions of
years. Selfish? Me? Boy that made me sore. He had
no right to say that. He just didn't.

I don't know how long it was that I sat in the back
pew of the church, but it was a very long time. The
votive candles were making a blur in front of my
eyes. On Saturday night, there were about ten people in line for confession with Kev. There were less
for Father Peterson across the way. He was easy in
confession. People said Kev wasn't so easy but that
he was good, that he would help you.

My palms were sweating. But I calmed myself.
Big deal, so I was walking inside a box and closing a
door. Nothing to be afraid of. I'd told Kev so much in

my lifetime, what was a little more telling?

Josh had been right, as much as I hated to admit it. I had to tell somebody. I had to unload it all on somebody or I'd go crazy. I was well on my way to crazy already.

I waited until the last person went into Kev's confessional, and started toward Kev's box. Soon the elderly woman who had gone in came out and smiled at me as she held the door.

She looked absolutely ecstatic. What had Kev said to her? Me, I was so strung out that I couldn't even smile back. I was shaking as I knelt down and closed the door. He was hearing the confession of the person on the other side. I waited. Then the door closed over there and it got silent. Only a moment's hesitation, then mine opened.

Too late to change my mind. I gulped air. "Bless me, Father, for I have sinned."

There was the hush of thundering silence as the blood pounded in my ears. I caught the familiar fragrance of his cassock with its mixture of incense and cigarette smoke. I sensed the nearness of him. My eyes were adjusting to the dark. Little pinpricks of light swirled in front of me. I could see, through the screen, the outline of one of his shoulders. I could feel, in the dark, the vibes of his uncertainty. But then I knew Kev enough to know he never spoke unless he was sure of himself.

"Go on," the voice was neutral, encouraging.

"It's been two months since my last confession."

"Hello, Brieanna."

"Hi, Kev."

"How are you?"

"I'm okay."

"I haven't seen you in a while."

"I know. I've been busy. How are you?"

"I'm hanging in. What brings you here? You didn't come here to say hello."

"I've come to confession."

Silence.

"I need help, Kev. I figured this was the best way to do it. You told me awhile back that any way I wanted to talk to you was all right with you. Well, this is the way I want to talk to you."

Again the silence. I knew he was thinking.

"Isn't it all right? That I'm here?"

"Yes, yes, of course. But I hope this isn't because you don't think we can talk outside. We can if you want."

"There's"—I sighed—"stuff I have to tell you, Kev, that I can't tell you any other way."

"Well, all right then."

"Do you want me to start now?"

"As long as you're straight about why you're doing this, yes. You can start anytime you want to."

"Well, do you suppose we could just talk for a minute first?"

"Yes, of course. Do this any way that's comfortable for you."

"Well, everything's pretty awful, Kev. Everything stinks."

"Just be careful now. This is a sacrament, Brieanna."

"Oh sure. Sorry. Everything sort of came down on my head all at once. I don't know how to tell you...." My voice trailed off.

He waited.

"First, though, I really feel bad for the way I've been treating you. I know I've been treating you pretty rotten."

"Are you confessing that? As a sin?"

"Yeah, well I guess so. Only I'm not sure what kind it is."

"Being rotten to your older brother? I'd say it's a very serious sin. Especially if he's been a good brother to you. Do you think he has?"

I felt something wrench and tear inside me. "I guess so. But I've really hated him sometimes too. And I've lied to him an awful lot. But that's nothing compared to the awful thoughts I've had about him."

"What kind of thoughts?"

I sighed. "That he's just too self-important some- times. And too superior to bother with me. And that he always thinks he has the answers for everybody else, but sometimes he doesn't even know what ques- tions to ask himself."

There was a silence on the other side of the screen, strained and too long for comfort. Then the voice

came, a little raspy but not angry. "Well now, maybe
he has been a little bit like that lately. I'm sure the
last part is especially true. But he loves you very
much and hopes you'll realize he's been under a lot
of pressure."

I felt everything loosening up inside me. "Do you
want to hear my other sins now?"

"If you want to tell them to me, yes. I'd be very
humbled to listen."

"Well, you know I've missed mass. A lot."

"Yes, I know that. But you have to tell me anyway,
even though I might know. It has to come from you."

"All right. I missed mass about eight times. And
I've hated God."

"You've what?"

"Hated God. At first, I was just pretty upset with
Him, because of something that happened lately. But
now I've decided I hate Him."

"Brieanna, do you know what you're saying?"

"Yes."

"Why have you hated Him?"

"I just can't stand some of the stuff He does, Kev. I
don't see the reason for it. It's all pretty stupid sometimes, if you ask me."

"Like what, for instance? What has He done to you
lately?"

"I have to tell you that later. I have other things to
tell you first."

"You can get to it whenever you want."

"Okay." I took a deep breath. "Every time I go to confession I have to tell this. And I don't really know how to tell you, Kev."

"Just say it, Brieanna. That's what I'm here for."

"Impure thoughts. I have them all the time. I can't help it. I think there must be something wrong with me. Sometimes my mind works just like an x-rated movie."

"Have you been doing anything to encourage these thoughts?"

"Like what?"

"You know what I mean. Have you been watching any more x-rated videotapes?"

"No. Honest, Kev."

"What about racy books or magazines?"

"Well, yeah, there's always those."

"What do you mean—there's always those?"

"Well, the kids at school have them. They pass them around. You know, *Playboy* and stuff."

"What do you expect your mind to do? What kind of fuel are you feeding it?"

"Well, I can't not look at them when they go around, Kev."

"Why not?"

"Because they watch me to see what I'm going to do."

"Why?"

I was trapped. I would have to be more careful. He'd trapped me. "They just do, Kev."

"Because of me? Because your brother's a priest? It wouldn't be because of that now, would it, Brieanna?"

"Yeah, Kev," I said miserably. "But it's no big deal. It's just that sometimes I do things just so they won't think I'm different."

"I see. I wish you'd told me about this before, Brieanna. You're going to have to get to the point where you don't take the bait, where you don't mind being different. Part of being an adult is having the courage to be different. As for your thoughts, you haven't told me. Do you take pleasure in them?"

"Well, jeez, Kev."

"Just answer the question."

"Well. Yes."

"All right then, that's the sin. Not the temptation, but giving in to it. Everybody is tempted. Do you understand the difference?"

"Uh huh."

"Answer properly now."

"You don't have to be such a prig, Kev."

"Brieanna!"

It got quiet. He was angry, for the first time. He calmed himself. "You came to me like this for the structure, the privacy, and the security of the sacrament. Now have some respect for the sacrament."

"Yes, Father."

"Don't call me Father. That isn't what I want."

"Well, jeez, Kev, what do you—"

"I simply want you to understand that this is different from outside. But you don't have to call me Father. As for your impure thoughts, don't dwell on them. Get your mind on something else. You have a good mind. And lay off the racy material. Go on now, you're doing fine."

"Well, there's the drugs, Kev."

Silence. I felt silence, like something palpable, like some living thing swirling around me in the dark. Then, "Why don't you tell me about the drugs, Brieanna," he said carefully.

Chapter 20

I could not answer right off. I could tell that he was thinking the worst, which is what older brothers do all the time with younger sisters. And, to be sure, he was being an older brother as much as he was being a priest. But his tone had been gentle, inviting and not threatening, so I took a deep breath and plunged in.

"Kev?"

"Yes. I'm here."

"I told you and Dad that I went to help Josh find the drugs that I hid on the island that night. You remember that."

"I remember." He sounded kind of winded.

"We didn't throw the drugs out, Kev. Like I said. Barry Buetell was there. He wanted to keep them. So I let him. I let him keep them on my island. I let him bury them there."

He cleared his throat. "Are you telling me the stuff was there all this time and you knew it?"

"That's what I'm telling you, Kev."

He was quick, I will say that about him. He accepted the fact of the whole thing, face value. He didn't shock or anything. And he went right into action, deliberating.

"Why did you do this?"

"Buetell asked me to."

"You did it because he *asked* you to?"

"Well, it was more like he begged. First, he threatened, though. He said he'd call the police and tell them there were drugs on the island if Josh didn't get me out there that day. He'd already buried them again where we couldn't find them. Only he needed permission to use the island. So he had to ask me. He said his pusher would do bad things to him if those drugs were lost or stolen. He said he had no place to keep them."

"Brieanna, that wasn't your problem. Didn't that occur to you?"

"Well, sure Kev. Only if he called the police, nobody would suspect him of having brought the drugs there. He's on the National Honor Society and everything. And all the other kids who were there would be in trouble. Would that have been right?"

He hesitated. "Remember what I always told you about the end never justifying the means?"

"Well sure, Kev, but it didn't mean that much. Because there weren't people involved. Now I know the kids involved. I didn't want them to get into trouble."

He was silent. "All right," he said finally. "Only one thing. That was the day we had the fight, wasn't it? You wanted to talk more, and I didn't have time and you ran off."

"I don't mean to be disrespectful or anything, Kev. But you were the one who ran off that day."

"Yes. Did the fight we'd just had enter into your decision to let Buetell keep the drugs there?"

Every nerve in my body told me to lie. But that would make the confession worthless. All this for nothing! He would know if I lied, too. He always did. "I don't remember."

"Well, think. We have time."

There was no way out. "I only know that I didn't care, right then, if he kept the drugs there or not."

"Why?"

"I was upset, I guess. Because we fought. I was sore at you. And disappointed in you that day. Because of what I saw...because of what I thought I saw between you and Diana." There, I'd said it. He had what he was after. I hoped he was happy.

"You did it to get back at me then."

"No. I didn't do it to get back at you. I told you the reason I did it, Kev. So the other kids wouldn't get in trouble. That was my main reason."

"All right. But it was still wrong. You have to take responsibility for that wrong."

"I do, Kev. I've been doing nothing but going crazy over it ever since."

"Why didn't you come to me? You do, in one way or another, whenever something is bothering you."

"I wanted to. I almost did tell you a couple of times. But I knew what you would have done while the drugs were there. You'd have made me report it, right?"

I could sense that he was smiling. I could tell by the tone of his voice. "I'd have gone with you to report it, but yes, essentially you're right. That's what I would have had to do if you'd come to me. I couldn't give you absolution otherwise. Now there's no sense in telling anybody. It wouldn't help your friend. It wouldn't make anything right for anybody. The sin lies with you, Brieanna, and you ought to make up for it."

"How?"

"I don't know yet. I'll think of something. Now is there anything else?"

"Yes." I was enormously exhausted. But there was something else, and I supposed I ought to tell him if this whole thing was to be valid. "I wanted to have sex with Josh."

He cleared his throat. "What do you mean?"

"Well, I don't know how I can say it any plainer, Kev."

"All right, I'm sorry. Give me a minute here. Did you?"

"No, but I wanted to all right."

"Well again, that's normal. As with the thoughts, it isn't sinful unless you do it."

"You don't understand, Kev."

"I do, Brieanna. Believe me I do."

"I asked him to. He refused."

I could feel his distress, his pain. The vibes were so obvious through the screen. "You *asked* him to? You certainly are full of surprises today, Brieanna."

"I know. I'm not what you always thought I was. I know you think I'm innocent and good."

"I never thought that. None of us is. And I speak from personal experience. But I just didn't think you were that sophisticated yet."

"Oh no, Kev. I didn't want to go all the way. I wanted to neck, that's all. I had a fight with him because he wouldn't. He wouldn't even kiss me. I can't tell anybody else this, but he never really has. And I have something else to tell you too."

"I'm listening."

"He's gay."

"Now, Brieanna, that's not a fair assumption."

"It's not an assumption at all. He is. He told me."

I could hear him breathing on the other side of the screen, it was so quiet. "He told you this?"

"Yeah, Kev."

"Honey, I'm sorry."

"He told me a couple of weeks ago. And I've been a zombie ever since. I haven't been able to tell anybody. And I don't know what to do. It's killing me, Kev, it really is."

"You're not going to cry now, are you?"

I wiped a few stray tears. "No, I'm all right. All I've been doing is crying."

"Brieanna, I feel terrible about this. I feel terrible that you didn't come to me in the last couple of weeks. And worse that I've been so preoccupied that I didn't come to see you."

"It's okay, Kev."

"Let me ask you a question. What made you decide to come to me now?"

"Josh bugged me to. He keeps saying he wants to be friends. And I can't. He says I look awful and I have to tell somebody. Because I won't talk to him about it. He said I should come to you."

"He's concerned about you."

"He said you'd help me, Kev. You gotta help me. I've done everything you wanted in here. I don't know what else to do." My voice broke and I wiped away a few tears. I had never, in my life, felt so wounded and vulnerable.

"All right," he said gently, "I'll try. What do you want to talk about first?"

I gulped. "Why is he like that?"

He didn't say anything for a minute. "Are you asking me why some men are homosexuals?"

"Yes."

"Nobody has determined that yet, whether it's in the body's chemicals or in the conditioning, in the psyche."

"But whatever it is, God did it."

I felt him smile through the darkness. "Yes. If you want to put it that way, yes."

"Well then, do you see what I mean about God? And the things He does? What's the sense of it, Kev?"

"Oh, Brieanna, Brieanna, you've really come to me with a tough one today." But I could hear his enthusiasm warming up as he began to talk. "We don't know the sense of it. Any more than we know the sense of a lot of things. It isn't for us to understand. I don't agree with the church's position on homosexuals. The church will never condone such behavior. But if the homosexual isn't practicing, there is no sin. Only if they practice their sexuality is it a sin in the eyes of the church. I have trouble with that, with denying a person their sexuality if they're made that way. But then I have trouble with a lot of stuff the church says."

"I don't care about the sin, Kev. I care because I can't talk to him anymore. I run away from him in school. And he keeps wanting to talk to me, to be friends like we were before. He keeps wanting to make it all right. It isn't all right. You gotta help me, Kev."

"I am. I'm getting there, Brieanna. Do you still feel the same about him as you did before?"

I didn't answer right away. I had to think about that one for a minute. It was something I hadn't allowed myself to consider before now. But Kev was making me consider it. "I loved him before. Now I hate him," I said.

"You wouldn't be talking like this if you hated him. You wouldn't be here. You're simply having trouble adjusting to what he told you. But it's obvious you still like him. It's possible you still even love him. He's the same person as before, isn't he?"

"I don't know. That's what I can't figure out."

"Of course he is. You fell in love with the person, not his ability to have sex with you. You fell in love with what's inside him. His mind, his personality, his offer of friendship. Has any of that changed?"

"No."

"Well, then, he's still the same. And he's asking for your friendship. Has he told many others about this?"

"He's told nobody but me."

"He hasn't given his friendship to many others either, from what you've told me. Once, you said you weren't sexy enough in his eyes, Brieanna. I told you then not to place value on yourself only through the eyes of a man. What I meant was, as a man sees you sexually. Obviously Josh wasn't doing that with you. He likes you because of who you are. Not as a sex object. You ought to be flattered."

Why wasn't I flattered or pleased? I wasn't. I couldn't think of an answer. I just knelt there listening.

"You're a fine person who has intellect and under-

standing and spirit and sensitivity. That's what Josh
saw in you. He didn't ask for anything else. And this
is what he wants from you. To see him the same way.
Without sex getting in the way. Can't you do that?"

I felt frustrated and confused. What Kev was saying sounded so wonderful, but what about the feelings I had when I was around Josh? What was I
supposed to do with them?

"What about if I wanted more than that from him?"
I asked.

"You'll have to settle for friendship. And fill those
other needs with someone else someday. Right now
it doesn't seem that you're doing so bad with Josh.
Did he ever lead you to think the relationship was
anything more?"

"No," I answered honestly. Josh hadn't. I had to
give him credit for that.

"Then you built up in your mind that it was more.
That's your fault. Sure, he should have monitored the
whole thing more carefully. But perhaps he saw
something in you that you don't even see in yourself
—the ability to love him in friendship in spite of
what he is. How did you act with him when he told
you?"

"I screamed at him, Kev," I said shamefacedly. "I
hit him and I cried."

"Oh, Brieanna," he said.

"Yeah, I know. I was pretty rotten."

"He opened his heart to you and you treated him
like that?"

"He only told me because I was pushing him to neck. I forced the issue."

"He opened his heart to you," he insisted firmly. "Do you think that was easy for him? Of all the sins you told me tonight, that's the worst. Are you aware of that?"

"No."

"Well, I want you to be aware of it. Lack of charity. He who hath not charity . . . are you so without sin that you can cast stones? What did Jesus say to the woman at the well?"

"Oh, Kev, don't give me that."

"I am giving you what you need to hear! I am giving you all I have to give you."

He was so certain in his anger.

"I'm sorry," I said.

"It's all right. I know you're confused and wounded. You have every right to be. But you don't have a right to judge him. Or hate him. You have a responsibility, as a matter of fact, to react properly to what he told you. You have a responsibility to try to see things from the good side of your heart."

"The what?"

He sighed as if I had missed some elementary lesson along the way in life. "We humans have a choice, Brieanna, all through life. We don't have much of a choice about what parents we're born to or what diseases we get or if we're homosexual or straight. Or if we have good looks or not. We don't have much to say about most of the things that befall us. The

choice we do get, the only real choice, is how we
react to what life dishes out to us. Are we going to be
bitter and hateful or are we going to take what happens and come through with courage and grace?"

He paused. Did he expect me to answer? I didn't,
and he went on.

"We have that choice. To become bitter and resentful or to see things out of the good side of our
hearts. And make life work for us. That's what you
have to do now. Forgive Josh, first of all. Then you'll
have to work past your own hurt and see him for the
good and decent person he is. I don't know if you
can do that, Brieanna, but I'd certainly like to see you
try."

He stopped. Still I didn't say anything.

"You need to work on that. Forgiving people. You
do an awful lot of judging, it seems to me. You could
do this with Josh. You could make up for your complicity with the drugs on the island by trying with
him, couldn't you?"

My voice was raspy. "I don't know, Kev."

"Oh, come on now. You two had a good thing
going, as I recall. All those trips up to the refuge to
see the animals? What about that? You had something good that you shared between you. Sex wasn't
the only thing, Brieanna. Your friendship went
deeper than that. Didn't it?"

"I suppose so."

"I certainly *hope* so," he whispered sternly. "I certainly hope you weren't just going around with this

boy for the sake of sex. That would make me very unhappy, Brieanna. A sexual attraction is fine. It's perfectly all right. But there has to be more between two people. And I think you and Josh had more. And that's what you have to try to focus on. What you shared with him before."

"But..." I stopped, unable to go on.

"But what?"

"He's so beautiful, Kev," I said. I didn't try to keep the misery out of my voice. I didn't care if he heard it or not.

He picked right up on it, of course. "Beautiful, is he? And how is he beautiful?"

"The way he's built. The way he holds his shoulders and his head. The way he smiles. I saw him once on the track outside school. He was running and he had his shirt off." My voice broke. "You don't know what I'm talking about."

"I know what you're talking about," he said evenly. "What makes you think that I don't know?"

I remembered Diana and was flooded with remorse. "I'm sorry, Kev. But what do I *do* about that?"

He sighed. "What you do is focus on the person, on his misery. His need for friendship. And what you share between you. And look to someone else for the rest, like I told you. I want you to try with this, Brieanna. I'll help you. You can come to me and let me know how you're doing. The hardest thing we have to do is love people when they betray us. God does that. When He isn't busy making the world miserable for you. I don't know if we humans can ever attain that pinnacle. Hate the sin and love the sinner. I've said that to you before."

"All right, Kev, I'll try."

He sighed. "I've been harsh with you. And you've been very good about it. And very dear to come to me like this. Have I helped you at all?"

"Yes, Kev, a lot. You're a good priest."

He grunted. "Now if there's no more I'll give you your penance. Say ten Our Fathers and ten Hail Marys. And pray for me. I need it. Now make a good act of contrition."

I was surprised to hear him say that. Pray for me, I need it. And I was strangely touched by it. I said the familiar prayers. My heart was bursting with feelings I'd never had before. My body was drained. I was relieved at what I'd done, not sorry. If for no other reason than to have been a party to something I'd witnessed here, some holiness in Kev I'd never really seen before. What I'd seen was the priest in him. And I knew one thing. He was good at what he did. He knew how to reach into the darkness in people and wrench the sorrow out. He actually fought a person to make them see things right.

I saw his hand making the sign of the cross, and I concentrated on my prayer. He was giving me absolution. I felt a rush of warmth and affection for him. He hadn't turned me away. He hadn't favored me either. But he had given me all he had to give.

I wiped my face with my hand and kept right on

kneeling there in the dark after he'd closed the screen. I was unable to move.

I don't know how long I would have knelt there. I felt like a tree after a storm. I'd been tossed about and stripped of every dishonesty I had but I was still there. It wasn't very long before the door opened, and he stood, framed against the light behind him, his stole around his neck. He smiled and held out his hand. "Come along," he said.

Chapter 21

He took my wrist and led me to the back of the
church. The church was empty. He slipped into a
pew. I sat down, while he knelt and prayed. He put
his face in his hands and was very quiet, kneeling
there for a while. There wasn't much left of me either, I can tell you that. So I didn't break his medita-
tion. I just sat there wondering what was coming
next.

He finished praying and sat back in the pew. For a
few minutes, neither of us spoke. I wasn't about to
volunteer anything. And then his words came in a
harsh whisper.

"I know I wasn't there when you needed me. Because of my problems. And I do have problems. I'd
like to tell you some things now, Brieanna."

I waited.

"I'd like to give you the same degree of honesty

that you gave me. You were right about me,
Brieanna."

"Kev, you don't have to—"

"Please be quiet until I finish. I...this isn't easy
for me. But I owe you this. I've broken my vows.
One of them anyway."

I know I stopped breathing.

"Aren't you going to ask which one?"

"No."

"I've broken my vow of chastity."

I felt my breath come out in a whimper. My head
started to spin. In front of me, the votive candles
dipped and blurred. But I said nothing.

"You see, Brieanna, I did know what you were talking about in there. And I'm telling you this because I
want you to know. But I...I've stopped. I mean
we're not seeing each other anymore. She's gotten
herself transferred to another area. I think she
couldn't handle being involved with a priest, once...
it happened. But you were right all along. I didn't
see what was happening. I made all kinds of excuses."

"Oh, Kev."

"I'm sorry if I let you down." He sounded so sad.

"You didn't let me down," I said.

"Yes, I did. I know how you looked up to me. But
I'm human, like everybody else. I was always so
proud of my track record on that score. I knew other
priests who were having problems with celibacy, but
not me. I was sailing along, invincibly. And then

Manuel came along, and I started asking questions.
What happened with him really shook me up. I
started slipping. It wasn't just Diana. I was losing it
already, Brieanna. I was questioning all my reasons
for my faith. Still, I didn't fall. Diana was there, and
I was tempted, but I didn't give in. That day we
fought, when I walked off with her? I want you to
know that I wasn't... sinning in that direction yet."

I folded my hands in my lap, listening. Tears glis-
tened in my eyes. I loved Kev a lot, but I don't think
I ever loved him as much as I did in the back of that
silent, empty church, when he confessed his sin to
me.

"I held off getting involved with Diana. Then one
day, when I was depressed and despairing, I turned
around and she was there. She was just there." He
shook his head. "And no Lutherans or Presbyterians
or Methodists were there to stop me, either. Like
when I loaned the hall to Manuel. I need to tell you
this, Brieanna. I can't have you thinking I'm this
saintly priest. Because I'm not."

"You're a good priest, Kev. I don't care what you
did."

His blue eyes looked at me. I could see the question in them until he satisfied himself that I was sin-
cere. "I wish I felt the same way, Brieanna. I just
don't feel that I am anymore. I feel as if I've betrayed
everybody."

"You made a mistake. Don't other priests break
this vow too?"

"Sure. Lots of them."

"Do they quit because of it?"

"No." He drew in his breath. "They confess it and go on. But I don't know if I want to go on. You see, it isn't only that. I'm fragmented, Brieanna. The trendy name for it today is burnout. That's my real problem. The affair with Diana is only a symptom. I really think this parish work did it to me. To see people who aren't poor needing me so much! I got so I wanted to hold back pieces of myself. Just for one person. And not be pulled apart. I couldn't take any more calls in the middle of the night with people dying, the marriage counseling, the constant dispensing of advice to middle-aged women. These people were all well-heeled and seemed to have everything together in their lives. And yet, when I got to know them, I realized they had more problems than my street people in Newark. I started resenting that. Another sin. No, I'm not cut out for parish work. And then Manuel sought me out, after knowing me in Newark, and I saw him as the one person I wanted to help, to focus on. And I wasn't allowed to."

He fell silent, and I gave him his silence. "Now, of course, I see that a priest has no right to feel that way. That the reason I was ordained was to give myself, in little pieces, to everybody. I don't know if I can go on doing that, Brieanna. I think I've lost the desire to."

I didn't know what to say. Why was he telling me all this? Did he expect me to help him? *Me?* I supposed that he did. He was still my brother. But what could I possibly say to make it all right? To make any sense?

And then it fell together in my mind, miraculously, like the pieces in a kaleidoscope. "Kev," I said tentatively, "Daddy told me he thinks it's about time you had doubts. He says everybody has them. He says ... who do you think you are, not having them?"

He just looked at me. The blue eyes were waiting. I went on. "Daddy says the one thing we all have to learn in life is what commitment really is." I cleared my throat. My voice was shaky. "That you may think you're committed to the priesthood, but that you won't really find out if you are until you're disillusioned."

I shut up then and looked to see how he was accepting this.

"Well," he said dryly, "I'm disillusioned all right. I guess you could say that."

I felt everything relax inside me, and I went on, braver now. "Daddy says that if you can have commitment after you're disillusioned ... well, he says you've got to have it if you're really gonna cut it with anything that's important to you. He said that anybody can perform when the times are good and you've got a good tail wind. He said ... try holding on to what you believe in when the rug gets pulled out from under you. That's when you know if you can cut the mustard."

I held my breath.

"He says that, does he?"

"Yeah, Kev." I stole a look at him from beneath my lashes, hoping I hadn't gone too far.

"And when, may I ask, were you two discussing me?"

"Oh, it was awhile back. When you first told me you might leave the priesthood. You were fooling then, but I got scared. I told him you were in trouble. He said he knew it. He said that you'd never been tested in your priesthood and one of these days you would be. And that's when you'd prove yourself a really good priest."

"I'm glad you two discussed me so thoroughly."

"Don't be sore, Kev. He says he knows you're a good priest. And a lot of other people know it too. But that you don't know it yet. And you have to find out for yourself. That it isn't anything anybody can give you."

"Well, he's right about that." He shook his head. "I wish it were as simple as he makes it out to be."

"You do?" I asked hopefully.

"Yes, I do."

I held my breath again and plunged in. "Well, couldn't it be?"

"I don't see how it can."

"Well, Kev"—the thoughts were falling nicely into place in my mind now—"isn't that what you were just telling me in the confessional?"

He looked at me.

"I mean, it's what you want me to do with Josh,

isn't it? To be committed after he disillusioned me?"

His eyes narrowed. "It isn't the same," he said.

"I don't see why not. It seems to me that one of us needs to stay committed to a person and the other to...to something you believe in. We've both been hurt, Kev. And we don't want to bother anymore. We can't see the reason to bother. Do you think either of us has a reason?"

He pondered for a moment. And I could see I had him. I had him cornered nicely, where I wanted him. I was using the argument he'd given me. And if he didn't buy it, then he couldn't stand behind what he'd just told me in the confessional. And I knew he would stand behind his own words. Because he'd believed them just a little while ago when he'd said them to me. That had been the real Kevin, the priest in action. Only he had to see it for himself.

He looked at me. The blue eyes were tired. And in them, I saw wariness and suspicion and belief and hope, too. But I saw more belief and hope than I saw wariness and suspicion. And that's why he was a priest.

"You've been listening to the things I've been telling you," he said.

I said nothing.

"All these years, you've been listening, haven't you?"

I shrugged. "I couldn't really help it, Kev. You talked an awful lot sometimes."

"And you listened. It's affected you, hasn't it, my being a priest."

"Well, geez, Kev, sure."

"For the better, I mean. It's rubbed off on you."

"I was stuck with it, Kev. I had to make the best of it," I said.

"I shouldn't do this."

"Do what?" I inquired innocently.

"I feel as if I'm bargaining here, with my priesthood."

"You're not bargaining. You're just standing behind what you told me in the confessional. I believed you in there. If it's true, then why can't you do what you said? You want me to."

"What did I say?"

"That we have a choice. That we can become bitter and resentful or react to what happens to us with courage and grace," I recited. He was studying my face, waiting. I went on. "That we can see things out of the good side of our hearts and make life work for us. You could make the priesthood work for you, Kev, if you wanted."

He half turned to face me in the pew. He rested his elbows on his knees and put his forehead in his hands.

"Kev?" I said.

"Yes, Brieanna."

"Are you sore? Am I out of line or something?"

"No, sweetheart, you're not out of line." His voice

sounded very muffled and far away.

"Are you all right, Kev?"

He picked his head up. "Yes, I am. I was just thinking on the fact that you're getting away from me, Brieanna. I make the mistake, constantly, of still thinking of you as a little girl. I can't do that anymore. I've got to watch myself."

I stared at him, and I could feel a rush of joy. I smiled. Did he know what I was thinking?

I was down. I was off that ladder finally. And somehow I knew I'd never be on it again.

"I just can't stand to see you throwing everything away, Kev, because you made one mistake. God allows mistakes, doesn't He? Even from His priests?"

He said nothing.

"You said I should forgive Josh. You said we have to learn to forgive people when they betray us. And that God does that kind of stuff. Well, wouldn't He forgive you then? I mean, not only your broken vow, but everything?"

He shook his head and knelt down again, only this time he reached for my wrist and pulled me with him. I knelt next to him, realizing that he wasn't saying anything because he couldn't speak. He put his face in his hands and prayed silently. I was very honored to be invited to kneel next to him then, because I knew something very special was going on with him at the moment. After a while, he finished. Then he cleared his throat and said this to me:

"I promise you. I won't do anything rash. I'll try my best. I'll try to stand behind what I told you in there. I'll give it my best shot, okay?"

"Okay, Kev."

"Now, I make a mean cup of hot chocolate. Wanna come to the rectory and have some with me?"

Chapter 22

"Brieanna?"

"Wha...what?"

"You've got company."

My father stood, all six feet two of him, long and lanky, in the doorway of my bedroom. Behind him, silhouetting his question mark of a figure, the light from the hall spilled into my room. I roused myself from my bed and blinked. I'd come home from my Saturday night hot-chocolate session with Kev at nine-thirty and fell promptly asleep on my bed. "What time is it?"

"It's ten-fifteen. She's with some boy downstairs in the living room. She said she'd come up if you'll see her. Just for a few minutes."

I rubbed my eyes and tried to orient myself. "Who?"

"Gina Falcone."

I was awake now, all right, pulled awake by the
incredibility of it. Gina? Here? A stab of alarm went
through me. What did she want? Josh? That was it,
something had happened to Josh. Wildly, I tried to
pull it all together in my mind as I stared up at my
father.

"Are you all right, Brie?"

"Yes, Daddy, I'm...is something wrong? Is that
why Gina's here?"

He came into the room. "I'm worried about you,
Brie. You look as if you've seen a ghost. What should
be wrong?"

"I haven't seen her in weeks. We don't talk anymore. We had a fight."

"Be that as it may, Brie. She's here. No, nothing's
wrong. She just asked very nicely to see you. When
Kev brought you home before, I thought you looked
kind of washed out. Shall I tell her you're not feeling
well?"

"Oh, Daddy, I haven't spoken to her in so long that
I don't know what to say!"

He started out of the room. He hesitated at the
door, and his long frame threw a shadow across the
floor. "You want my advice, Brie? Are you asking?"

I looked at him standing there, so hesitant and cau-
tious and...I searched my mind for a word and then
it came to me. Respectful, that's what he was, of my
feelings. He wanted me to see Gina, I know he did.
But he wasn't going to say so unless I asked him. I
saw him as I'd never seen him before that instant as

he stood in the doorway of my room. My father. The guy who stood back, while Kev and I had made all our mistakes. Who always sensed when something was wrong with his kids yet was hesitant to intrude. Oh, he was a parent all right, and he let you know it when you did something wrong, but lately, it seemed that he was waiting to be asked for advice instead of giving it so readily. He was doing an awful lot of standing back these days, and waiting. On the sidelines.

And yet it had been his words that came out of my mouth tonight when Kev needed words. His philosophy, which I'd made my own. And which had worked for me. And for Kev.

I smiled up at him in the lamplight. "You think I should see her, Daddy? Even though we fought?"

Once the question was put to him, he'd answer it, of course. Even though he tried not to look pleased that it was put to him. "I think you should, Brie. You grew up together, you know. If the girl has something to say . . . well, I don't know why you fought. I'm not asking that. But I think you should see her, yes."

I got up. "Maybe one of these days, I'll tell you, Daddy," I said.

"Well, that would be nice, Brie. If you want to."

"I can't yet. But I can tell you this." I stumbled around trying to find my slippers. "I think everything's gonna be okay with Kev. I mean, we had a long talk tonight. That's why I was late coming in."

He nodded. "I'm glad," he said.

"Maybe..." I hesitated. "I can't tell you all about it, Daddy. But I can tell you"—I took a deep breath and started again—"you helped me, Daddy. To say the right words to Kev when he needed them."

"I did?" he was incredulous.

"Yes. Tonight, when we talked. I think I said the right words. But I couldn't have said them, Daddy, if not for you."

"And what were those magic words, may I ask?"

"Not magic." I shook my head solemnly. "I don't even know if they worked. I think they did. I mean, I think they got him thinking in the right direction. It was just something you said to me once that popped into my head when I was talking to him tonight. About commitment after disillusionment."

He scowled. "That's pretty heavy stuff. I didn't think you accepted it at the time when I said it to you, Brie."

"Well," I shrugged and grinned. "I guess I did. And I hit Kev with it tonight. And I really got him thinking. I just want you to know."

He nodded. "Well, I'm glad I'm good for something around here." He started out the door. "Shall I tell your friend to come up?"

"Yes. And thank you, Daddy."

He looked at me. Our eyes locked. "Anytime," he said.

I was sitting on the edge of the bed when she came in. She was in jeans and a bulky knit sweater and

ankle boots. The light behind her in the hallway
made a halo around her hair.

"Hi." She didn't smile or anything. She looked
uncertain. And thinner, if that was possible.

"Hello yourself. Come on in."

She came in and sat down in a chair across the
room, and for a minute, we just looked at each other.

"You found out," she said, "about Josh."

I nodded, yes.

"I know you must hate me. The way I acted toward
you. I didn't know what else to do. I tried to stop
you from going out with him."

"Why didn't you just come to me and tell me about
it?" I asked softly.

"My parents won't let me talk about it. To anybody. They've sworn me to secrecy." Her face was
very white. She stared at the floor. "I knew about
Chittendon. I knew what really happened there. So
do my parents. Only they won't talk to me about it.
They won't even talk about it to each other. We're a
great family, aren't we?"

I didn't know what to say to her.

"We're all walking on eggs all the time, trying not
to admit it or hurt each other," she went on. "And
we're all screaming out, inside, to talk about it." She
wiped her nose with her hand.

I got up and handed her a box of tissues.

"Thanks," she said. "Anyway, I'm sorry you were
hurt. I know you liked him and I'm ... sorry."

I nodded.

"I tried to warn you. Because you were my friend. But you wouldn't listen."

"I...just wish you had talked to me about it, Gi. Weren't we good enough friends for that? I would have kept it quiet. That's what hurts me the most, I think. That we were friends, and you couldn't talk to me about it."

"Don't you *understand?*" she asked. "Nobody is allowed to talk about it in our family. I know you don't understand, because you're so open in your house about things. You all talk all the time. About everything."

"Yeah, I guess we do," I agreed.

"Anyway, that's what I came over to tell you. That I'm sorry you got hurt. And I'm sorry I couldn't warn you. And I'm sorry we fought."

She got up and started to go. I had to stop her. I sensed her pain, I sensed how difficult it had been for her to come to me like this. And I knew in my bones that if she walked out, without my saying anything, we'd probably never speak again. I couldn't let her go!

"Gi?"

"What?"

"I'm glad you came over."

She smiled weakly.

"I'm not sorry I went out with Josh." I started to blurt it out without thinking. And once I started to speak, it was as if it all fell into place. As if I was finding out something about myself that I hadn't known before. "I'm not sorry. If you'd told me, well, I don't know if I would have gone out with him. Probably not. And I still feel bad that you couldn't tell me. But in a way, I'm glad that it turned out this way. That I got to know him, I mean. I really mean it, Gi."

Sometimes we have to hear ourselves verbalize things before we really know how we feel. And she'd done that for me tonight, coming over like this. She'd pulled those words out of me.

"You mean it?" she said.

"Yeah." I got up and walked toward her. We stood looking at each other in the soft glow of my lamplight. "I'm not sorry it happened. Any of it. Josh and I are going to be friends. We are friends. We haven't ... I mean, I haven't seen him in a while, but I'm going to see him in school on Monday. And tell him that. He's been waiting to hear that from me. He's left it up to me whether I want to be friends or not after he told me about himself. I've decided I want to."

"And you're not sore at me then? For the way I acted?"

"Well, you did act pretty rotten. But I haven't exactly been so great this fall either. I ... I've missed you, Gi. I've been a real pain to everybody. You don't know some of the stuff I've done."

"Like what?" Her eyes widened.

I shook my head dismally. "Oh, some real off-the-wall stuff. I've been lying my head off to my dad about things and sneaking out and getting away with it. I've been lying to Kev too. Up until tonight anyway. I thought I was getting away with everything. Kev said I always come out standing on my feet. It looked that way for a while. But then it all caught up with me."

"How?" I could tell she was intrigued. And I started to realize just how much I missed our confidences.

"Josh," I said simply. "I was sneaking around with Josh under my father's nose. Doing lots of other stuff too. And I never got caught. And then Josh caught up with me. I mean, I found out about him and..." I shrugged. "I didn't get away with anything at all, Gi. Nothing," I said flatly.

She leaned against the doorjamb. "I missed you, McQuade. I know now how much. How long's it been since you had a decent, calorie-loaded sundae at the Blue Cupboard?"

"Too long," I said.

"I hear your dad's getting married."

"Yeah."

"Well, anytime your stepmother gets too much for you, you can sleep over at my house, okay?"

"Okay," I said.

She slipped out the door. I sat back down on the bed, staring at the empty doorway, wondering if it had all happened or if I'd dreamed it.

* * *

The school week that started Monday was the week before Thanksgiving. The weather turned raw and cheerless, and teachers were giving tests as if their jobs depended on it. I did some last-minute cramming Monday and Tuesday, and I guess everybody else did too.

Twice, I sought Josh out. I went to the *Close Call* office at lunchtime, but it was locked. I know they were in there. I heard the typewriters going like mad. I knocked once. Sebring, the editor, came to the door.

"Yeah."

"Is Josh in?"

"He's on the phone. Doing an interview. We're on deadline. You got something for us?"

"I . . . no."

"You're McQuade, aren't you? You were writing for us."

"I'm not anymore."

"You were good. Why did ya quit?"

"I got busy."

He nodded. Why was I flinching under his gaze? Seniors intimidated me, everyone except Josh. "You oughta come back. We could use you around here. We're short-staffed. Maybe next semester. Think on it."

I felt a glow of pleasure. "I will. Thanks."

"You wanna hang out and wait? We keep the door locked, because the girls hang around. Like groupies. But you're different. You can wait."

"No, really." I backed away. "I'll come back when he's not so busy. Just tell him...no...I'll come back later."

"Suit yourself," he said.

Tuesday I tried again. Each time it took courage. My knees were actually shaking by the time I got to the *Close Call* office. My palms were sweating. The second time, I found the door locked again, only I didn't knock this time. The paper was due out tomorrow, the day before Thanksgiving.

The next day, Wednesday, we were dismissed early. It was cold and snow flurries were swirling outside the windows at school, and a current of excitement about the holiday and the snow traveled through the corridors all morning. A final bell rang somewhere in the hallways, echoing in my head as I made my way to the *Close Call* office. The door was shut again but not locked. The paper had been distributed that morning. I tried the knob, turned it, pushed the door open a bit. The place was a mess with copy on the floor and coffee cups and cigarette butts strewn all over the desks. In the middle of the mess was Josh, leaning back in a chair at the far end of the room, his feet resting on the bottom drawer of a desk. He was reading the paper.

He didn't hear me. At least, he didn't look up from his reading and that reminded me of the first time we'd met right in this very room. That day, so long ago, when I'd come in with my essays in a brown manila envelope and he sat reading them without looking at me.

How handsome I'd thought he was. Instant attraction. Was that only a little over two months ago? It seemed like years.

"Hi, Josh."

He looked up and smiled. "Hello."

"The paper looks great."

"It's improving."

My eyes went over him, the slim but muscular figure, the straight shoulders in the Oxford shirt, the pencil resting on his ear. Some stab of remorse flooded through me as I looked at him. All that handsomeness, all that masculinity, wasted. I wanted to cry. I wanted to throw things around. It was as if I had double vision, looking at him. First I'd see the Josh I'd known, the one I'd fallen in love with. Then, right before my eyes, that person would dissipate into nothing and this other person would be there. A Josh I didn't know. A stranger.

Which one was real? Could I ever merge the two? Why was it that everything Kev had said to me made so much sense the other day, but now it all seemed stupid and inadequate?

"I'm glad you came." He pushed some papers aside on the desk and got up to pull a chair over. "Come on, sit down."

I approached the chair as if it were rigged with an

explosive device. "Are you sure you're not too busy?"

"'Course not. Hey, you want a soda or something?" There was a machine out in the hall.

"No, thanks. This place looks like a bomb hit it."

"It always looks this way when we get a paper out. Doesn't your dad's newsroom look like this?"

"No. I mean, he has computers."

"Yeah, well he's also got money coming out of his eyeballs."

"And he's got a competitor right across town."

"How you been, Brie?"

"Okay. I've been fine."

"I'm glad. I've been thinking about you. Even in the middle of the last couple of days and all this. Honestly, I have. I've been hoping you were all right."

"Yeah. Well, I am. I'm great."

We sat there in awkward silence for a minute. He looked down at the pencil in his hands.

"How's Sinbad?" I said.

"Oh, great. He misses you. And the geese, too. We got a few more of them last week. They took them in from the golf course now that the weather's turned cold. They'll keep them for the winter."

"Are you going to the homecoming game tomorrow?" I asked.

"I gotta go. I gotta do a story for the paper." He shrugged and smiled, and his eyes crinkled at the corners. My heart dropped ten feet inside me. "You know how I feel about football. It doesn't really turn me on."

"Me neither."

"You going to the game?" He looked at me.

"Well...," I shrugged, "We always go in our family. My dad and Amanda. Even Kev."

"How is he? Kev?"

"He's okay. I mean he's going to be okay."

"Did you have a talk with him?"

I nodded my head. I was finding it increasingly difficult to speak. I held my breath for a moment, and Josh picked up on my mood. He leaned toward me and reached out and touched my hand in my lap, then withdrew it quickly.

"Brie, I want to hear anything you want to say to me right now. I'm sitting here afraid to breathe, if you want to know the truth. Because I might say the wrong thing and you'll run away."

I nodded. From somewhere down the hall a bunch of kids came past the *Close Call* door, joking and laughing. They passed and the sounds receded. Everyone was leaving. There is nothing in the world more unnatural than a quiet school. Josh and I smiled at each other weakly.

He was waiting. I drew in my breath in an attempt to control the emotion in my voice. "Josh, I wanted to tell you that it's all right. That's what...I wanted to tell you. But I can't do that. It still hurts."

He nodded.

"I know..." I took another breath and continued. "I know that you didn't lead me on or anything, that ...um...that all you ever said was you just wanted to be friends. I know it was my fault that it got this far with me. It was a dumb-kid thing to do. But I couldn't help it."

My heart was racing. I couldn't look at him. I sensed movement on his part. He sat forward, leaning toward me. His face was very close to mine.

"Brie."

I wouldn't look at him.

"Brie." I sensed he was smiling. He reached out and put his hand over mine. "Hey," he coaxed, "look at me."

"I don't think I want to," I said.

"But I want you to."

I looked. Can eyes be sad and smiling all at the same time? His were. "Brie, it wasn't your fault. It was mine. I had no right to put all that on you. I wasn't honest with you. I needed your friendship desperately, and I took a chance and it backfired. And you got hurt."

"It'll be okay," I said.

"But you're not okay. And there isn't anything I can do to make you okay. Is there?"

"You can be patient with me. I want to try and get it all right. I don't know if I can do it right though. But we can be friends. Like you wanted."

"You still want to be?"

"Yes." It was true. I did want to be. I wasn't lying

to myself. Kev had told me that I had to be careful of lying to myself. That if I chose to be friends with Josh, I might always start hoping he could change. I must never, Kev had said, hope for such a thing. The friendship must be unconditional.

Of course, it wouldn't be easy. I knew that. Did I want to be friends with somebody who had eyes like his? A physique like his? Looks like his? Did I want all that in front of me when it was just a pretense? When it all meant nothing?

But who was to say what meant anything in life and what meant nothing? You could go with a great guy who'd hold you and kiss you one minute and not be there the next. For the distance, for the bad times as well as the good, for the times you needed talk and sharing, Josh would do. He would serve me very well.

Forever, he had said. Even after I was married.

I felt everything relaxing inside me. I could go out on a date tomorrow night and find somebody to kiss me if that's all I wanted. But where would I find another Josh? Where would I find somebody who wanted to be friends without any strings? With no price tag.

I smiled, even while tears came to my eyes. "I still want to be friends," I said again. "I'd be ... most honored to be friends with you, Josh."

"I knew I could count on you, Brie. I knew, all the time, that you were more than the others. I took a chance, but I knew you'd understand."

I nodded and gulped. He brushed my hair from my face and gave me a handkerchief. I wiped my eyes and my face. "I look awful," I said.

"You look beautiful to me. How about"—he checked his watch—"how about we take a little ride up to the refuge. And wish the animals a happy Thanksgiving."

"I'd love to."

We both stood up at once. "Before we go out of here today, there are some things I'd like to say to you, Brie," he said.

I waited.

"First, I wanna thank you for coming here like this. I've been so miserable these last couple of weeks. Things haven't been easy for me. Especially since I left Chittendon. You're the first person who's really been nice to me."

I was going to start crying again if he went on like this. He went on.

"Second, I want to thank you for accepting me the way I am. My parents haven't been able to. My sister has, but she tries to keep the whole thing a secret. I understand. It's what my parents want. I feel I can be myself with you and not pretend. You don't know how good that is."

His blue eyes were shining with tears.

"Look, there's one thing you have to promise me. We can be friends, but you have to go out with other guys. You can't just hang out with me. I can't have that."

I nodded.

"If you don't have a date and you wanna see a movie or you need help with homework, I'm here. But I don't want you giving up dates on account of me. All right?"

"All right."

"And it would be nice if you let me take you to the homecoming game tomorrow anyway."

"All right," I said.

"Look, I can help you if you have any problems with guys. You can tell me. I'll advise you how to handle the creeps in the future."

"You sound like Kev."

"No, I don't wanna take his place. We have something special. I don't know exactly how to define it yet. But we'll settle into something and figure out what we are to each other. We have time." He grinned. "And it doesn't mean we have to see each other all the time either. I only have one semester to go, and then I go to college. But it doesn't matter. We can write. And we don't have to stifle each other. You and me, we don't have to do that. You understand?"

"I think so."

And then he did something I'd been wanting him to do for two months. He put his arms around me. I was surprised at how natural and good it felt. I leaned my head on his shoulder for a minute, and I felt a surge of affection for him that didn't need any summoning and wasn't contrived. "Oh, Josh," I said.

"Hey, it's gonna be okay." He released me and smiled. "Let's close this place up now. Let's go and visit the animals."

Epilogue

The ceremony went so fast. What was it, seven minutes? Can you believe that someone can actually get married in seven minutes?

I stood in the front row of the municipal court in the town hall, next to Kev, surrounded by all the people who came to see my dad and Amanda get married by Mayor Parker. It was not my idea of a place to get married, although they did try to make it look nice, with the track lights in the ceiling beaming down and the flowers and the guitarist Amanda had hired to sing. There was a brown spot in the ceiling of the courtroom from where some water had recently leaked in. Standing next to Kev, I couldn't help wondering what he thought of the whole thing. I sensed he felt out of place in his priest's clothing.

And then I thought, good. I hope he feels out of place. I hope it bothers him. Because that means he's still very much a priest after all.

My dad certainly looked handsome. Not many men of fifty-three can cut as fine a figure as he can. And, of course, I don't have to tell you how Amanda looked in her pale blue lace dress. The person who shocked me was Amanda's dad. He isn't much older than my father. But why not? Amanda is only thirty-four.

Actually it wasn't such a bad ceremony. Everybody I knew came, and being as it was the Saturday between Christmas and New Year's, the flowers were poinsettias, and the whole town hall was decorated with white lights that sparkled when we came out afterward. Everyone certainly was in a festive mood to begin with.

My heart lurched for my dad as he stood there accepting congratulations in the reception line afterward. And my heart lurched for Gina and Josh when they came over to me and both kissed me. There's a brother and sister team for you! She looked smashing in her blue silk dress. And I don't have to tell you how Josh looked. My dress was plum velvet. Amanda helped me pick it out, and I got a lot of compliments wearing it.

Josh. I watched him on the sidelines. He looked so handsome! And then I pushed the thought aside, out of my mind. He looked across the vestibule of the town hall and winked at me and told me to line up with my dad and the rest of the family so he could get a good shot of all of us together. Of course, Dad had Teddy Ferris, the photographer from his paper, taking the formal shots because Ferris does weddings as a sideline. But Josh was taking pictures for me. He'd offered to. He's good at photography, too, I found out. Is there anything he isn't good at?

Our house positively glowed for the reception. Alma and Amanda and I had worked hard to pull it all together. Dad had helped, too, and Kev and I went and ordered the cake and the food.

The house was full of Christmas lights, of course. And the tree was still up. Amanda had outdone herself decorating. Dad had given her a free hand to do whatever she wanted, and I had a lot of fun helping.

After the reception, Kev and I were leaving too. We were taking Dad and Amanda to the airport and going on from there to a ski lodge in Vermont. We had two rooms reserved. Dad was paying for it. I was delighted, of course. Dad had told me he was doing it for Kev, because Kev needed a rest and a vacation. He told me I should look after him and make sure he got some rest.

I know he asked Kev to look after me too. He probably told Kev that I needed to get away so I wouldn't feel lost or abandoned after he got married. And that Kev was to see that I had a good time.

My father didn't know about Kev and Diana. And he didn't know about me and Josh. I'm sure of that. But the thing is, he didn't have to know. He knew enough, which was that both Kev and I had been through our share of sorrow lately and he wanted us to get away. I loved him for it. And I was happy for him and Amanda. He deserved all the happiness in the world. And I kissed him at the reception and told him so.

"I'm a lucky man, Brie," he said. "I've got a wonderful woman and two great kids." He told me then that I meant a lot to him, and that I was never to feel dispossessed because he and Amanda had gotten married. And that he would always be there for me when I needed him. Sometimes I ache inside thinking how much you can love a person. And that the more you love a person, the more your heart can break.

Kev said he wouldn't babysit me at the ski lodge as long as I touched base with him every day and had dinner with him at night. And as long as I didn't question him either. Of course, I agreed. I didn't know what Kev had planned. With him, it could be anything from having a drink at the bar to skipping off into town to say mass at the local Catholic church.

He wouldn't be dressed as a priest at the ski lodge, of course. When priests go on vacation with regular people, they don't do that. It would make everybody uncomfortable. And I wasn't to blow his cover, either, he told me sternly. He had permission from his superiors for this vacation. They knew he needed a rest. They were giving him time to get away and do his thinking.

How do they know you'll behave, I teased him. Of course I still tease him about stuff like that. He wouldn't want it any other way.

"They know I'm going with my teenage sister," he said. "How can I not behave?"

When the wedding reception was going on at our house, I had packed already. Had my skis ready and everything.

The night before when I was packing I found the gray sweatshirt Josh had given me. The one that said Chittendon.

I didn't know what to do with it when I came across it in the drawer where I'd stuffed it away. I held it up and looked at it and cried. I just sat there on the floor holding it, fingering it. It was so soft. And the colors were so military. It was like Josh. It was all he was and all he couldn't be. I cried for a while sitting there holding it. Because I still do cry a lot about him. Every once in a while, it all settles over me and I can't help it. I just cry.

And then I folded up the shirt and put it in the bottom of my overnight bag.

I'd wear it. I figured I would wear it under my ski jacket where nobody could see it. There next to me. Like my feeling for Josh. I would wear it when I was flying down the slopes.

DATE DUE			
MAR. 2			
APR. 2			
APR. 27			
MAY 4			
DEC. 8			
APR. 14			
FEB 2 5 '97			

5448

F
RIN

Rinaldi, Ann.

The good side of my heart.

**ST. ANNE SCHOOL
BETHLEHEM PA.**